When your brain constantly runs 100 miles an hour, you might as well put it to good use. And when you have a tattoo above your heart that says "storyteller"—then get to it. And that's what B.L. Berg has done with her debut novel, *Lady and the Tramp and Me.* For her inspiration is everywhere, and nothing can become absolutely everything when she's sitting behind the laptop.

Visit her at:
Facebook.com/BLBergAuthor
Instagram.com/BLBergAuthor

Also by B.L. Berg
The Dream Maker and The Candy Cane

Inspired by:
Woolly, the Old English Sheepdog
Fido, the mongrel
Melly, the mongrel
Tyson, the German Shepherd
Barcelona, the Great Dane

B.L. Berg

LADY AND THE TRAMP AND ME

AUSTIN MACAULEY PUBLISHERS™
LONDON • CAMBRIDGE • NEW YORK • SHARJAH

Copyright © B.L. Berg 2023

The right of B.L. Berg to be identified as author of this work has been asserted by the author in accordance with sections 77 and 78 of the Copyright, Designs and Patents Act 1988.

All rights reserved. No part of this publication may be reproduced, stored in a retrieval system, or transmitted in any form or by any means, electronic, mechanical, photocopying, recording, or otherwise, without the prior permission of the publishers.

Any person who commits any unauthorised act in relation to this publication may be liable to criminal prosecution and civil claims for damages.

This is a work of fiction. Names, characters, businesses, places, events, locales, and incidents are either the products of the author's imagination or used in a fictitious manner. Any resemblance to actual persons, living or dead, or actual events is purely coincidental.

A CIP catalogue record for this title is available from the British Library.

ISBN 9781398437852 (Paperback)
ISBN 9781398437869 (ePub e-book)

www.austinmacauley.com

First Published 2023
Austin Macauley Publishers Ltd®
1 Canada Square
Canary Wharf
London
E14 5AA

Recently a friend of mine asked me how I come up with stories and honestly, that's a difficult question to answer. Mostly, it feels like my brain thinks it's home alone and decides to throw a party. It then proceeds to invite all sorts of people and creatures to stop by at every hour—day or night. Sometimes I don't even know about the party until after it has happened and I get to clean up the mess. But it's a fun mess. So many random thoughts, so many notes on my phone, scribbles on post-its and random pieces of paper. It is a patchwork of thoughts and ideas—and in the end, it becomes a story.

At some point, most of my friends have experienced that my eyes have glazed over and I've grabbed my phone to take notes or started scribbling on the nearest paper like a maniac. Thank you so much for your patience.

If I don't mention two of my fiercest supporters by name and get them a numbered, signed copy of the book—preferably number one and two, of course—I'll get into some serious trouble, trust me! So here you are: Susanne, you always listened with true dedication. You shared my annoyance, frustration, and excitement like it was your own. Lene, you were—and still are—my go-to. The person who always answered texts when I was freaking out and needed confirmation that what I was doing not only was a good idea, but it was the right thing to do. The only thing to do. The thing I should do. And it was justified I felt brave. At some point you must have stirred that witches' cauldron in the right direction. Thank you for that.

This book wouldn't have happened without the Editors at Austin Macauley who read the story and decided they really liked an ugly dog and strange people. It was a big day for me in September 2022 when they told me they'd like to publish *"Lady and the Tramp and Me"* —I almost felt like I'd been accepted at Hogwarts. No owl could have made me happier. Thank you for this opportunity.

Also thank you to the team who helped realise everything—particularly Ruth, the Acquisitions Editorial Assistant, who must be the nicest, most patient and most helpful person on planet Earth! My point of contact: Jack and James, who coordinated and kept track of everything, and the team behind them.

The story wouldn't have come to life either without the dogs I've owned and known—so thank you for the inspiration. I used to be a dog owner myself, so I know all about dog owner madness, the eaten shoes, and the walks in the rain on cold, dark nights. I miss it so much.

For now I only have Tramp—and I'm very happy to share him with you. More chaos is coming.

Table of Contents

Blissfully Ignorant: An Introduction	11
Collateral Damage	21
Vetting	42
Not Bloody Pongo	55
About Ten Square Feet	66
Coffee to Go	79
A Dog's Life	95
The Angry Woman	102
Furry Cockblocker	116
A Lot of Teeth	132
Unexpected Visitor	140
Miss Marple Land	152
Singing Chipmunks Can Drive You Insane	160
Great Expectations	169
There Is No Heaven—Probably Not for Dogs Either	178
Houdini Has Fur	188
The Good, the Bad and the Ugly	198
Apparently, Miracles Happen	208

Blissfully Ignorant: An Introduction

Did you know dogs can say 'fuck you'? I didn't. Not until my grandfather was on his deathbed and he made me promise I'd take good care of his puppy.

"Promise me, you'll take good care of my puppy, Simon." His eyes were teary and full of regret as he reached out and held my hand. I suspected the tears was mostly an act and the regret was a partial tribute to Sean Bean when Boromir dies. My grandfather was never the emotional type.

"When did you get a puppy?"

"A few months ago. Please take care of him," he pleaded. I loved my grandfather, I really did, and I'd do anything to make him happy, but a puppy…It didn't quite fit my lifestyle. Honestly, it didn't fit me in any way.

"A puppy? Come on, I can hardly take care of myself." I meant it slightly as a joke and also as nice way of letting him down. I didn't want a puppy.

"Simon, please. He'll be all alone if you don't."

"Where is it now?"

"My neighbour Mrs Getty is watching him."

"Can't it stay with her?"

"She'll take him to a shelter," my grandfather said horrified. Yeah, I had just about the same idea. I might be the worst grandchild in the history of the world.

"How about Ben and Margot?" Surely my sister and her obnoxious husband would be the better choice.

"Ben's a prick," my grandfather snorted, and I couldn't really argue with that one. "Please, Simon."

"Okay, I'll take the puppy. I promise."

"Thank you. Thank you for not letting him end up in a shelter," he smiled happily, and I got the feeling I'd just been had. And that's how, I was to become a dog owner in the very near future by a dying man's last request.

When people say 'puppy,' you expect a cute, little thing, don't you? Something fluffy, and furry, and soft, and looking like either some creature Disney made up, or something on the bottle of fabric softener, right? I call bullshit on that one, because reality is something entirely different, I found out. Reality…it's bloody brutal.

My grandfather died and was buried—you usually do that—and Mrs Getty was kind enough to keep the puppy for about a week. I wondered what would happen if I didn't pick it up, but in the end, guilt made me do it anyway. Yeah, you heard me—guilt. Not decency, not to be nice, not because I made a promise, not because I loved my grandfather—just plain old guilt. I don't need to tell you I regret it, do I?

Mrs Getty sounded alarmingly pleased when I called her and told her I'd come get the puppy.

"Is three o'clock, okay?" I asked.

"It's fine, I'll just cancel with my daughter."

"You don't have to do that, I'll come by tomorrow instead."

"No, it's fine," she said *very* cheerfully—and a little bit strained. That should've alerted me, that something was not right, shouldn't it?

I don't know Mrs Getty, but I know *of* her. Her garden and house are always picture perfect, and if you're even slightly messy this place will give you either an anxiety attack, the compulsion to mess something up, or put a naked garden gnome in her front garden where everyone can see it. I'm leaning towards the anxiety attack as I walk up the path to her front door. I wipe my hands on my beige slacks, but the dread has more to do with the puppy I'm bringing home than anything else.

When she opens the door, I give her my signature smile— the one that makes women feel flattered regardless their age. Children think I'm a prince from fairy tales, teenagers blush, women my own age get horny, and older women turns cougar. Super human good looks, I've always had them. But Mrs Getty doesn't respond to my charm at all—there is definitely something wrong with this woman.

"Hello, Simon, come in." She makes a gesture towards the door mat, and I take care to wipe my feet before I enter. I wonder if she would refuse to let me in if I didn't? If I don't come into the house, I won't bring the puppy home—I should definitely have considered this earlier.

"Thank you," I lie and follow her into the living room.

Do you know the movie "Harry Potter and the Order of the Phoenix from 2007? It's the fifth in the Harry Potter series and it is—of course—based on J.K. Rowling's book. This movie's top bitch is Dolores Umbridge, a British Ministry of Magic Bureaucrat, and Senior Undersecretary to the Minister for Magic. She is played by Imelda Staunton, and the character is described in detail with full bio on the Harry Potter Fandom wiki. In the movie, she had the most horrid pink and prim office covered in cat decorations. Mrs Getty's living room reminds me of Umbridge's office, only it's yellow—not pink—and there are no cats but poodles instead. But it's equally nightmarish and I probably have as many goosebumps as Harry Potter did when he entered Umbridge's office for detention. Then again, I'm probably not as brave as Harry Potter." He was, of course, portrayed by Daniel Radcliffe—you know this, right?

Not only does Mrs Getty have plates and decorations with poodles. She also has two live ones, and they bare their teeth at me from the couch. They should probably be cute-looking all groomed and brushed, but the snarling makes me feel like they're really just stuffed animals waiting to kill you. Neither Cujo nor that Gremlin thing has anything on these two, that's for sure.

I don't feel comfortable turning my back to them and I glance over my shoulder as Mrs Getty leads me through living room. She stops in front of a door and unlocks it with an ominous click like she has just opened the gates of hell.

"Can't you take the puppy?" I ask.

"I'm sorry, no. I'd leave it at a shelter, and I know that's not what your grandfather wanted." Nice job rubbing it in, making me feel guilty—and here I thought Mrs Getty was at least a polite woman.

"Is this really a good idea?" I ask sceptically.

"Dogs are loyal, they have faith."

"Are you certain, there's no other way? I'm a stranger to it." Hear me trying to squirm my way out of it? Well, it doesn't work third time either.

"It's only six months, Simon. You have plenty of time to bond," she says far too cheerfully—like she's telling me it is *so* delightful hell is warm. She opens the door to the mudroom and points. "It's in the corner," she says and steps aside.

I take a deep breath before entering the mudroom. I tell myself to stay calm. It can probably smell fear.

I look for a small, cute puppy, but that's not what I see in the corner. The *thing* is shaggy and dirty-looking even if I'm certain Mrs Getty doesn't allow *anything* dirty into her house, not even the mudroom. It's a marvel my dirty mind even made it inside. The *thing* is huge for a puppy—lanky, grown Labrador huge—and it's really scruffy. I'd expected some tiny thing that'll make me look like an idiot carrying around and dressing up because the sodding thing is too small to keep warm on its own, and too small to keep up with my long strides. And there's another possible Disney moment for you: a cute puppy in a sweater—probably with hearts on it or something. But this looks like *nothing* Disney would've drawn—unless it was a *very* bad day, and he was in the middle of a drug-infused psychosis. The puppy's paws are disproportionally larger than the rest of it. So are the ears. Its head also looks too large for its body, and it almost looks like something you draw either as a caricature or simply to be cruel. Disney had *nothing* to do with this unless he used his left hand. I'm telling you.

"What the fuck is that?" I ask.

"The puppy."

"You're joking."

"No." She looks at me apologetically like it's her fault the puppy looks like...hell if I know what it looks like.

"Is that really a puppy?"

"It's a big boy."

"No shite."

"His name is Henry."

"Henry," I say lamely. Mrs Getty pats me comfortingly at the arm.

"I'll leave you to it." And then she leaves me in the mudroom—really fucking fast—with the scruffy, huge puppy who's looking at me like I'm a Martian and it's not quite sure if it believes in aliens or not. She locks the door behind me, and that's not really a good sign, is it? This might very well be the story of how I died.

I take a deep breath and squat down.

"Hey, Henry..." I coax, but the puppyish *thing* just looks at me like I've told it I got a nice cabbage treat in my pocket. It knows it's a carnivore, and it's *not* buying it. Here's the first 'fuck you'—I'm certain. It doesn't look intimidated either—only like I'm some kind of retard that shouldn't be out in public without my appointed nurse. After ten minutes, I sit my ass on the floor. I've been cooing Henry about a million times with no reaction besides a sceptical look. It probably thinks I'm as stupid as I feel, but I want the puppy to come to me and not chase it around the room. I know shite about dogs, but I can't imagine that'll be a good idea.

After another five minutes, I give up and I just talk to it. I've never had a dog and I have no clue what the hell I'm doing. By the look of the puppy's face, it knows too. Smart fucker, isn't it?

"My grandfather just died. He was your owner. He left you in my care," I tell it.

Blank stare.

"My name is Simon."

Doesn't give a shite that's for sure.

"Puppies are supposed to be cute; you know?"

Yawn.

"You're too shaggy-looking to be cute."

Cock of the head. Like I've said the first interesting thing during the last fifteen minutes where I've made a complete fool of myself.

"If you had a cute lady friend, you wanted to fuck, you'd look like the Tramp."

Cock of head to the other side.

"Really?"

Stands up exited.

"You're bit young to fuck, aren't you?"

Curious look.

"Or do you like looking like a tramp?"

Exited bark. More like yip-yip, but hopefully it'll be able to produce a decent woof when it's older.

"Tramp, is that it?"

A clumsy puppy-run—wow, it really is a puppy—and then I'm torpedoed in the chest. I let out a humph, because the so-called puppy has a skull like a sledgehammer. But at least somebody didn't take advantage of my grandfather and sold him an adult dog. That's something, isn't it? Or not. The older the dog is, the sooner it will die.

"If you're going to be *my* dog, you should learn it's better to fuck than look like a tramp," I tell the puppy.

Sceptical look.

Maybe it's *not* smart after all.

I spend half an hour in the mudroom with the puppy. It doesn't react to Henry at all but seems to think Tramp is a terrific word. So be it, I don't give a shite right now. It can sit, lie down, and bark at command. It can also wag his tail and most of his body like a pendulum gone amok. It also turns out very capable at pissing my pants while I'm sitting at the floor. I guess that means I'm sort of his property now as well. Either that, or it has just marked me as the biggest idiot in dog history and it wants other dogs to know too.

I look around the mudroom and it would seem like Mrs Getty has kept the puppy here for a while. It has an old, worn blanket in the corner and an empty metal bowl I assume should contain water. There are tiles on the floor, the walls are bare and depressing, and it looks like the room is under construction. There are scratch marks on the door like it's been trying to get out—all in all this room looks like a prison. No wonder the puppy was a bit sceptical when it saw me. To the puppy I probably looked like yet another jailer.

I knock forcefully on the door and only seconds later, the door is unlocked like Mrs Getty has been lying in wait for me right outside the door. She only opens the door until has enough room to stretch her arm towards me.

"Secure it with this," she demands and holds out her hand, handing me a rope. She watches me through the crack of the door and only when I've tied the knot on the puppy's collar does she open the door and step into the mudroom. If I didn't know better, I'd say the puppy was giving her the evil eye.

"Where are we going?"

"Out the backdoor," she says urgently as she unlocks it and almost propels me out the door. I'm almost surprised she didn't kick my ass too to ensure a quicker exit. It's raining outside and that doesn't make my day any better at all. The puppy seems nervous but also like its happy being outside. It promptly lifts its leg and pees on a garden statue of—you guessed it—a poodle. The puppy looks a bit shaky standing on three legs, but it manages to keep its balance and, my dear Mrs Getty, let me tell you something on behalf of the puppy: Fuck you. Mrs Getty puckers her mouth angrily, but she doesn't say anything.

What I assume are the puppy's toys and things are standing beside my car in a soaked cardboard box, and I sort of feel sorry for the ugly puppy. Nobody seems to want it except my grandfather. My father told me I was an idiot for taking the puppy. He didn't think much of my promise, and my mother looked sceptical too. Margot made a wager with her obnoxious husband, Ben, on how long I will last as a dog owner. Ben's family has had a dog once, and—according to him—that makes him pretty much an expert. I have absolutely no idea what my sister sees in him. Neither do our parents.

There're papers in the box too and everything looks sogged. I glance unhappily at Mrs Getty who's grabbed a raincoat *and* an umbrella *and* is standing beneath the overhang.

"He likes the unicorn," Mrs Getty says and points towards the box by my car. I want to snap at her why the hell wasn't it in the mudroom then, but I don't. I need to get the hell out of here because this woman grates on my nerves. No wonder her poodles were bitchy.

I go to the car and look in the box standing beside it. The unicorn is ugly as hell. It's pink and got red hooves and mane. It's got three-coloured horn and wings, stitched-on closed eyes, and a smiling mouth. The puppy carefully pokes it with its nose and then cowers a bit when it looks at me, like it's afraid it's done something wrong. This puppy is ugly like hell, but I still feel some kind of sympathy for this unwanted creature. Just like I can't help I'm so good-looking, neither can the puppy help it looks like someone made a tremendous mistake creating it.

I open the front door to my car and the ugly puppy looks tentatively at my sportscar before it puppies up and crawls into the floor by the front seat. It looks at me timidly with huge eyes filled with apprehension before it carefully takes the unicorn, I hold out towards it. It lays his legs on it like it's using it for comfort, and that's when I decide I need to get the hell out of there before I yell at Mrs Getty for neglecting the ugly puppy. I might not know shite about dogs, but I don't think she has been treating it like she should.

Mrs Getty hands me a large plastic bag for me to sit on in the car. My pants are drenched, and it looks like *I'm* the one who pissed my pants—not the puppy. Clearly, it's a prick and I swear I see it smirking when I complain loudly about the wet spot of piss.

As I drive home, I almost laugh hysterically. I have dog piss on my trousers, I have miscellaneous items scattered in the boot, because of course the cardboard box was so wet, it fell apart when I tried to lift it. On top of that, I now own an ugly puppy I have absolutely no idea how to handle. I might be interested if the middle p's was replaced by s's—that I do know how to handle—and I'm not talking about the furry kind of pussy here, you know?

Collateral Damage

Fun fact: According to the National Geographic, dire wolves were real—and even stranger than we thought. I'm a believer.

It's been about a year since I brought Tramp home to my apartment. Mrs Getty, by the way, is a liar. The creature was nine, not six months old, when I got him. I don't know why this seems important to me, but it does! His weird appearance gave him a lot of pity—particularly, the first few weeks when he was constantly carrying the unicorn around, and honestly, I've milked it. My neighbours in general have been very patient with both of us: he was a sad, scruffy dog-ish thing who was shite out of luck because I was his new amateur owner. I think he also got a lot of pity because he was ugly and not puppy-cute like Mrs Albert's Golden Retriever was. Before it grew up, before it bit the janitor, before her husband got the dog in the divorce, before she started drinking, and before she became a weird cat-lady. Now everyone in the building feels sorry for her too.

Tramp also got a lot of fans when he snarled at a shabby, suspicious-looking man lurking around the entrance of the building and scared him away. I haven't mentioned to anyone it was my friend Hugh—he always looks like that by the way—and he was playing with Tramp when this happened. Nope, not a word. We live on pity and fake bravery.

I now know why Tramp is so happy about the unicorn—he's humping it. And the unicorn just lays there and takes it with closed eyes and a smile on its face. Tramp has grown—a lot—the unicorn has not. When he was a large puppy, it looked almost decent when he was humping it—now it looks more like he's violating it like some kind of sick paedophile and the unicorn's eternal smile makes it look really dirty. That might also be why Mrs Getty didn't let him have it while he stayed with her, and now I hate her even more because she was definitely smarter than I've been.

Now I also know why dog owners go crazy and talk to their dogs. I know why they treat them precisely like humans. It's because it's very hard not to. And when you're single and living alone…it's impossible. Tramp knows all about my work, he knows all about me, what I like, what I don't like, what I think of the news and I talk to him about what's in the local paper.

"You see the this?"

Quirked eyebrow.

"It's really great."

Roll of eyes.

"They're finally doing something about the empty lot by the old cinema."

Lays down with a demonstrative loud thud—clearly not impressed.

"*Finally*, a proper place to park the car."

Rapt attention. Standing up again.

"Multi-storey car park, that's excellent."

So interesting. Wagging of tail.

"What did I say?" Shite, I said, "Park."

He runs into the hallway and returns with the leash in his mouth only moments later.

"I didn't mean it."

Scowl.

"I need five minutes."

Deeper scowl.

Guess we're going to the park—like right now!

I've already given Tramp almost every human characteristic I can think of. He scowls, he understands, he smiles, and rolls his eyes at me. He's fucking annoying, and if he really was a human, I would've punched his face long ago. Repeatedly. I don't care about punching another man, but hell no, if I'm hitting my dog even if he's far more annoying than anyone I've *ever* met.

I have no doubt he understands a lot of words and knows the way I'm feeling to some extent, but I talk to him like he's my human friend, like he understands every single word completely—I'm pathetic. At least I know it. Not all dog owners do.

He's gotten more control of his body—his tail is still a wild card though. But at least it no longer takes him fifteen minutes of whining and acrobatics to get his ears back to normal when he's turned them inside out sneezing. It took me a while to figure that one out. And when I did figure it out, I might as well admit I didn't help him. I just let him entertain me with his struggles. Once, when I had a few friends over, we even made a bet about how long it would take him to get his ears back to normal…Matt won, but he cheated, because he has taught Tramp to shake his head on command. Fucker.

Tramp and I have become quite a pair—at least I like to think so. He's my partner in crime whenever my upstairs neighbour is playing music too loud or too late. I start my own concert by howling and when Tramp joins in it totally drowns out the music. It's even better when my next-door neighbour who's a large, grumpy, sailor-looking fucker almost smashes my door knocking.

"Your dog's making a racket," he grunts when I open the door.

"I know, I'm so sorry," I wince. "It's because of the music," I say and point towards the ceiling where the loud thumping evidence is almost making my ceiling lamp swing. The neighbour pats Tramp on the head with his huge, meaty fist before he stomps towards the stairs. I snicker as I listen to my grumpy neighbour when he easily shuts down the party upstairs and I practice high-five with Tramp. I've read somewhere it's important you activate your dog and teach it useful tricks. With his size, I might unintentionally be creating the next Mike Tyson, but I don't think that's considered useful. Tramp is yet to bite somebody's ear of—at least as far as I know.

Other important commands:

"Tramp, look sad." Very useful when we're going for distress or pity, seeking forgiveness because owner's an idiot and it's all my fault.

"Howl." Very useful when driving the upstairs neighbour insane because he plays loud music.

"Shut up." Very useful when we're done driving the upstairs neighbour insane because he plays loud music.

"Whimper." Very useful when pretending we're sorry for something. We're usually not.

"Eat." Very useful when creepy neighbour from across the hall leaves disgusting post-it on your door.

"Enough." Very useful when I need to stop Tramp from doing *whatever* the fuck he's doing.

*

Once I had a ceiling fan. I don't anymore. Yes, you heard me correctly—a *ceiling* fan. The definite downside of having a huge dog is your own lack of imagination. Every time you think something is out of reach…it's not. I had noticed the fan had started creaking, I'd also noticed Tramp's growing interest, but, honestly, I hadn't considered he'd move in for the kill. He black-outed twelve apartments when he jumped, attacked, and tore it down. I found one blade bitten in half and another had been stepped on. Besides that, he hadn't shown it much interest—maybe he just decided he didn't like the noise?

Anyway, I pretended Tramp had nothing to do with the power failure and I discarded the remainder of the ceiling fan in my parent's bin next time I visited, because I couldn't risk anyone finding it in the garbage area at my own apartment with Tramp's pawprint on it. The only good thing about the blackout was that someone became aware of the illegal electrical installation in the entire building. But the downside—because there's *always* a downside when Tramp's involved—it was expensive like hell getting it fixed.

As expected, there was a lot of damage to my interior before Tramp settled—it took about a month and an endless number of magazines, pillows, shoes…It was either death by teeth, weight, or especially tail, and once something was flying through the air, it was open season. His most spectacular stunt was actually recently. His tail swept an innocent and unsuspecting plastic container with mayonnaise of the table and as soon as it was air-born, he chased after it. Before I even got my ass of the couch, he had caught it, bitten it, and shaken it to death by breaking its neck. There was mayonnaise splattered on the floor, the walls, and probably a lot of other places I didn't know and will never find out. I confiscated the plastic container, but for once let him roam the living room licking the floor and walls and…wherever he found mayonnaise. It's got to be the only time he's actually made an attempt to clean up after himself. He also started humping the couch, but I don't think that got anything to do with mayonnaise. It probably had to do with me washing the unicorn. It was covered in mayonnaise, and I couldn't stand the thought of him licking and sucking it for hours. Wash the unicorn, lick its face, hump it—that sounded so dirty *I* almost got a hard-on.

That incident was a pretty good narrative of how Tramp's brain seems to work-if it's moving, it can be chased. If it can be chased, it can be eaten. And everything can be humped.

"You are such a bastard."

Duh. Obviously.

"Asshole," I grumbled and for a second, I swore he was looking over his shoulder, like he was trying to understand what his bum had to do with anything.

So, collateral damage is to be expected. However, what I did not expect is his size. He might have been a big puppy, but that's nothing to the dog he's becoming. Jon Snow, your dire wolf is going to look like a pussy when this one's fully grown—I'm telling you! And just to be clear: If you don't know who Jon Snow is, our relationship ends this very moment.

I started socialising Tramp almost as soon as I got him home, because the whole dire wolf thing is only funny, as long, as Tramp doesn't actually eat anything living which might be missed by someone. Socialising him also meant socialising me with other owners and let me tell you something...dog owners...they are not of this world.

One man told me his dog was allergic to any dog food known to man *and* dog. I wondered how long that dog would have lasted, if it lived in the Middle Ages. I didn't wonder that out loud, though—that would've been dangerous. Believe me. A woman told me her dog wouldn't eat anything that wasn't mixed with gravy, tuna, or remains from their dinner—and we're not talking carrots here. I told her:

"Lady, if he's hungry enough, he'll eat a couch." That comment didn't make me any friends at all, and it's safe to say Tramp is better at socialising than I am. Thank God, he likes other dogs and so far, I've been spared the daunting task of rescuing...anything living really...that's gotten caught between his teeth.

I've also been told I'm a bad dog owner because if Tramp doesn't want to eat what I put in front of him, I figure he's not hungry and I remove the food after a while. Do you have any idea how bad canned dog food smells? If you don't, then consider yourself lucky because it's bad. Really bad. I'm not letting it stink up the apartment—Tramp's breath is bad enough when he's just eaten—and when you look at it, it's even worse. I spent the first month struggling not to vomit every time I opened a can. Obviously, Tramp doesn't want to starve himself to death, so he eats—I've got a *really* smart dog. Even smart enough to recognise it's eating the scented candles that makes him fart loud enough even to frighten himself. Sadly, his farts didn't smell of lavender—very disappointing since his farts usually smells like rotten eggs. But at least I'm rid of most of the candles, which was a cruel gift from my sister because she not so secretly delights in annoying me. Tramp stayed the hell away from the last two candles—told you, he's smart. I threw them out anyway because I really hated them. I blamed Tramp of course because I occasionally I can be smart too.

Also, Tramp now genuinely dislikes anything that smells of lavender, and whenever he's at my sister's, he does what he can to kill the lavenders in the garden by pissing on them constantly. My sister is not pleased, which means I definitely am, and I might even praise him in hushed tones whenever he pisses on the lavenders and my sister isn't listening.

Tramp doesn't like lavenders, but he likes the park. He likes plunging himself into the lakes, scaring the shite out of ducks and geese, even if he's not supposed to do that. I swear I can see him grinning every time he emerges from the muddy water. And he grins even wider when he's shaking himself off in front of me, drenching me with dirty water and seasonally tadpoles and algae. My dog's an asshole. To all of you, who thinks cats are assholes…I'll see your cat and I'll raise you one monster dog.

We've done a lot of training. I might be a reluctant dog owner, but no way do I not have my giant, ugly monster dog under control. Like right now, for instance, I'm standing alone in the middle of the park, because as soon as I took the leash of him earlier, he bolted like his ass was on fire. That hasn't happened yet, but he's been close a few times and the apartment has smelled of burned dog fur. This was before he ate the candles.

Did I mention it's five o'clock Saturday morning? Did I mention it's not even sunrise? It's May and bloody cold, because it's overcast, and I'm only wearing a jacket and pj bottoms because of the ungodly hour? Did I mention I had a few friends over last night, and we had beers and played cards most of the night? Well, I did, and I hate my dog right now. I'm so tired and frustrated I hardly notice the female runner passing me when I call out again.

"Tramp!" I yell and the woman screeches to a halt. She's looking seriously pissed when she turns towards me.

"What did you just call me?"

"Not you, my dog." She looks around, and then she looks at me sceptically. I don't blame her—I really don't—because there's no fucking dog anywhere in sight! There're not even any people besides the two of us.

"Who calls their dog Tramp?" She's clearly incensed, and I'll bet she doesn't believe a thing I'm saying. And it's not going to get any better.

"He named himself."

"Of course, he did, considering he's not here."

"You'll know when you see him."

"Him and the pink pony he's with."

"You think that's where he's at?" I ask with ironic excitement. I'm not exited, I'm pissed. Why the hell didn't she keep running like any normal person on the planet would have done, when you meet a crazy person yelling in the middle of the park wearing a pj? This woman is a bitch—that's why.

"Very funny."

"Do I look like I think it's funny?" I snarl. "I'm hungover, I'm tired, I'm wearing pj, boots, a jacket and nothing else. It's not even six in the fucking morning, I'm freezing my ass off, and your bubbly personality isn't helping shite." God damn it! I look around in the park, which is deserted, and when I turn towards the woman again, she's looking at my groin. "What the fuck are you doing?"

"You weren't joking about only pj," she snorts—I'm not amused.

I walk around in small circles looking for Tramp and calling out for him. I try to ignore the woman who's still looking at me despite I must act like a crazy person—or maybe she's looking because of it. Come to think of it, my striped pj probably makes me look like I've just escaped an asylum. She should definitely have kept running.

"I'm leaving your ass here, Tramp," I yell furiously at the empty park. "What you're doing is illegal, so do your own fucking thing. I'm going home." I'm just about to turn and walk away when I hear a rampage from the shrubbery, and only seconds later, Tramp comes crashing into the path and heads straight for me in a staggering speed. No no no no...He doesn't give a shite I weigh about two hundred pounds. Momentum, enthusiasm, and stupidity is enough for his hundred and twenty-five pounds to knock me on my ass when he barrels into me. He'll make an excellent rugby-player when he grows up.

The leash flies out of my hand, and I land on my ass on the gravel path with a thud, but at least I manage to tense my abs when he delighted stomps both front paws on my stomach like he's practicing CPR. I have no idea why he does this, but right now, I'm just thankful he's not jumping up and down like that on my balls.

"Sit," I wheeze, and Tramp happily plants his ass in the gravel.

"Oh my god, are you okay?" The woman asks. She's looking down at me and she's actually holding out her hand like she's got any chance of helping me get up. She's probably about hundred and forty pounds—a lot of weight is at her tits, and it's not good for balance leaning over and getting me on my feet. If I took her hand she'd probably topple. Then she'd end up on top of me, and then I'd be reminded of how long it's been since I've had sex. Angry woman or not, I'd fuck her in public in the middle of the gravel path busting my knees, with Tramp as an audience, if she was up for it. A man can dream and I'm that desperate, I shite you not.

I imagine having a dog is pretty similar to having a baby. You're tired, cockblocked, and in a state of constant worry about what could possibly go wrong just because you leave the thing home alone for eight hours. You walk endless miles to get the sodding thing to sleep, and when it eats it's all over the place. The laundry basket is always filled and it's expensive like hell.

However, there is one important difference: babies don't chew on a woman's thong making her leave you only seconds before penetration when she discovers it's being used for a chew toy. Babies don't howl sympathetically while the woman is shouting something about perversion and disgusting animal sex. Almost eating her soaked thong is hardly sex, but what do I know? Another difference: babies don't wag their tail while you're standing naked in the hallway with only your hands to cover your bollocks while you're loudly begging a sexy blonde to come back, swearing you'll make it up to her any way she'd like. And babies don't sit down on their ass with their lipstick dick sticking out when your old neighbour with his cane, Mr Roberts, opens the door to see what all the commotion is about.

"Simon, what are you doing to your dog?"

"Not a God damn thing."

"What did she say about animal sex?"

"The dog just ate her thong." Mr Roberts looked down the hall where Celia was stomping off in her criminally short skirt. Then he shrugged.

"So what? I would too if given half the chance."

Right now, Tramp is wagging his tail happily again despite my scowling—but at least his lipstick dick isn't sticking out. I get up on my own and brush gravel of my hands and look at him. The idiot has retrieved the leash, and he holds it in his mouth like a peace offering like he's a *good boy*. He isn't. I often wonder what exactly my grandfather managed to teach him before he passed away, because sometimes Tramp does some very strange things. And before you say anything—no, it's not fucking cute! He couldn't look cute if someone paid him a million in doggy treats.

"You're an asshole," I tell him as I take the leash. I grumble as I put it on him and turn towards the exit with him trotting happily beside me like he didn't just tackle me to the ground and attempted to pump my stomach.

"Your pj's ripped," the woman calls out just as I feel a draft over all of my left ass cheek and my butt crack.

"I don't give a shite, I've got a great ass," I shout without turning around.

When we get back to the apartment, I go straight to bed. It's Saturday, it's still not even six o'clock, I'm *not* supposed to be awake by now. I've turned my back to the bedroom door, I'm lying close to the wall, naively hoping to escape Tramp. The fucker has the neck of a giraffe because he seems to be able to reach me anywhere.

I've closed my eyes and I'm relaxing—I want to sleep. But I only get three minutes in peace before I hear the tell-tale sound of huge paws shuffling across the floor. Then a paw on the bed.

"No dogs in bed," I grumble.

A whine and I hear his paws against the rug as he's eagerly tapdancing on the spot beside the bed.

"I mean it," I say with my back still turned.

A humph.

"Until you stop licking your balls, don't roll in dead animals, and watch what you're stepping in, the bed is *off limits*."

Whimpering.

I'm not giving in on this. I might be a guy, I might not consider it necessary to clean *very* often, but even I have a sense of basic hygiene and *my* cock will be the only one leaking in my bed.

"Simon says no," I growl and he stops tapdancing. One day, when I lost my temper, I told him through clenched teeth about Simon Says, and it basically meant he had to do what the fuck ever I told him to—right now! I don't know if he could sense I was about to lose my shite, or if the phrase just appealed to him like the word tramp—but none the less it worked. I only say it when I'm *really* frustrated. I figure there's only so many precious times I can use the phrase with the desired effect—therefore I'm saving it.

Tramp pokes my naked ass, where my pj is ripped, with his snout, and he's got to be one healthy fucker because it's cold like an ice-cube.

"Jesus, Tramp," I yell as I practically leap of the bed. My body is in total shock because of the cold imprint on my ass.

Smug look.

"You're a menace," I grumble.

Looking proud.

"Do you really hate me that much?"

Enthusiastic bark. That can mean just about anything.

"Maybe I should let Ben dog-sit you for a weekend?" I threaten.

Growl.

"*Then* you'd miss me."

Sceptical look and then he flops down on the floor and roll onto his back.

"I'm not buying it. You'll never look cute."

Surprise.

"If you had to wake me up, couldn't you have made coffee?"

Roll of eyes.

"I'll make you a deal. I'll feed you if you learn to make coffee."

Fuck you. Really. Fuck you.

"You seem to be able to do anything you set your mind to."

Smug look.

"Why not coffee?"

Blank stare.

I'm certain he ignores me on purpose and I go to the kitchen to make my own damn coffee. When the coffee is ready, and he's slobbered his breakfast, we go to the living room. I turn on the TV and watch the news while I'm sipping the coffee, and Tramp settles on the floor. He's not allowed in the couch either, but he seems to accept this more easily than the bed. This doesn't stop him from occasionally working his bum up on my lap until he's practically on top of me. I'm sure he's trying to be discreet, but he's too heavy for that. Believe me, there's no mistake when Tramp is sitting on you.

I have no idea why he easily accepts he can't sit in the couch. I have no idea how his brain works. Period. Maybe it's because he considers the TV like some kind of unpredictable enemy I need to be protected from. He still hasn't forgiven the TV for when I watched Jurassic World. The Indominus Rex would be shite out of luck if it ever wanted to eat me, that's for sure. Whenever it growled, Tramp's hackles rose and he stood up prouder and fiercer than ever, and the snarling he made was hardly the sound of a large puppy—it was that of a predator that meant business.

Tramp has mixed emotions about the TV. He stands between me and monsters and alien movies. News and dialogue in general are boring except a few words—I haven't figured out which—that stirs his interest. He likes Animal Planet and I swear he goes through every emotion watching it. For some reason, he likes the sound small animals and kittens are making, and it's been one hell of a struggle to make him stop licking the screen. He howls with the wolves, and he looks at the TV like it's speaking a language he doesn't understand when whales are singing. It's sort of funny to watch and I often look at him more than I do the TV. The downside—because there's always a downside to anything regarding Tramp—is I've had to stop watching porn with the sound on. Anyway, he's pretty much the reason I pay for Animal Planet—told you dog owners are crazy.

He doesn't like the sound of politicians in general and treats them the same way he treats Godzilla and Indominus Rex, but that's not a problem. It's slightly more problematic he doesn't like Ewoks either. Ewoks are cute, right? Everyone likes Ewoks, don't they? Even if the noises they make are slightly annoying. Still, he bravely stands between me and the TV whenever there's *any* kind of monster on TV. I guess he likes me after all.

*

During the past year, I've also learned there's a lot of competition among dog owners. Everybody think their dog is special. Previous dog owners are even worse, and the memory of their dogs tend to be just a tad too amazing. My brother-in-law Ben is one of them. Whenever I bring Tramp to my sister and brother-in-law's place, we have a man-to-dog talk in the car before we enter the house.

"Tramp, this is important. Behave."

Whine.

"I mean it."

Grunt.

"Ben is annoying and even more if you don't behave."

Smug look—I've got you by the balls.

"He's going to insist on training you."

Disbelief.

"And I might just let him."

Whimper.

"It's all up to you."

Fuck you.

"You know my sister's nice."

Scepticism.

"Come on, you like me too sometimes."

Huff.

"Really? That hurts Tramp."

Roll of eyes.

"You don't like me at all?"

Yawn.

"Not even when I feed you?"

Shrug.

"Walk you."

Shrug.

"Wow, really?"

Roll of eyes.

"You know I'm proud of *you?*"

Raises head.

"You're looking for a bribe to admit you like me?"

Smug look.

"You're an asshole."

Manic wagging of tail.

The first time I brought Tramp, Ben just looked at him. Then he huffed, because he had had a dog when he was younger, and that dog was something beyond special because it was a Dachshund. Apparently, they are notoriously difficult, and worst of all…the owners relish it. And talk about it. And brag about it. Apparently, having a difficult dog can be 'a thing' for some people. I don't get it, but perhaps those people still have their sex-life, their ceiling fan, and their sportscar—just to name a few things.

Every time I go to my sister's, Ben spends the first fifteen minutes asking me the same questions, he asks me every time. I think he does it because he's a condescending prick, but also because he wants to make sure to point out my dog is a loser because it's not a purebred, is not called something fancy, is not cute, and so on. Little does he know I don't give a shite. Besides, I've had Tramp long enough to become immune to annoying things—compared to Tramp, Ben's just an amateur.

"What species is that again?" Ben asks as soon as the front door is closed behind us.

"A lot?"

"So, it's not a pure-bread?" Ben huffs like purebred is a good thing. I've learned that some dog owners pay an obscene amount of money for a pedigree which sometimes only is a guarantee for recessive disorders because of inbreeding. It's said mixed-breeds dogs are healthier—if that's true Tramp will probably outlive me, because that's one mixed-up dog. Yes, I do mean mixed-up.

"Not even close."

"Why was it you call him Tramp?"

"He responded."

"Come here, Tramp," Ben says and claps his leg. Tramp just stares at him. "Come on," Ben urges and here it comes...the 'fuck you' as Tramp sits down by my side looking up at me like he's asking me to please, please, *please* let us ignore the man calling his name. Again.

"Oh, that's so cute," my sister says. Tramp rolls his eyes—I'm certain—but he still shuffles to my sister, so she can pet him. My sister is five-feet-eight and no small woman.

On top of that, she's pregnant and weighs about the same as a full-grown blue whale. Despite that, she steps a bit to the side as Tramp leans against her and I see her surprise. He's a heavy fucker and he's getting bigger every day. I'm big too, but I have a niggling feeling Tramp will outgrow me. And probably outlive me too. Not sure I'm going to trust him with any kind of caretaking when I grow old.

I think Margot likes Tramp, but his size can make any sensible person hesitant. By pain of death, I'm not admitting I think my sister is sensible, but she's not altogether stupid.

"We can't have him running round the house, Simon." Margot looks worried like I will find it offensive she is worried about Tramp. She shouldn't be, because I understand completely. Contrary to me, she loves her knick-knacks and there'd be nothing left of it if Tramp was let lose. Even I have a limit for punishing my sister. Besides, I'd never hear the end of it from our parents.

"Fair enough," I say easily, and I truly mean it.

"Come, Tramp," Ben demands and heads towards the garden door while Margot heads for the kitchen. Tramp glances at Ben—fuck you—and then he happily trots after Margot. Ben looks like he's just has had his first taste of lemon ever, and Tramp raises his tail in further triumph.

"Oh," Margot says happily, when Tramp bobs her hand with his snout to call attention to himself. Again. "Are you looking for a treat before you go to the garden?" Tramp wags his tail and I'm certain he's doing his best to look adorable. He fails completely of course, but he gets a treat anyway—I suppose that's why he keeps trying.

We're having dinner when I hear shuffling of very huge and very familiar paws and there's only a moment before

Tramp appears in the door leading to the patio. Margot is sitting with her back to the patio, Ben is across from her, and he frowns when he sees Tramp.

"Uhm…Margot, why didn't you tie the dog up?"

"I did," she says, looking confused.

"Then why on earth is he stranding right behind you?" Margot turns and Tramp sits down—I swear there's suddenly a halo over his head. He doesn't manage to look the least bit angelic though, but nice try. "You haven't done it properly," Ben says irritably, standing up. "I'll do it." He grabs Tramp by the collar, and I glance warningly at Tramp. He'd better follow Ben. Just in case, I stand up and follow Ben and Tramp into the garden. "A bowline knot will do the trick," Ben says arrogantly. He grabs the rope and ties it around Tramp's collar. I swear I can see Tramp thinking 'fuck you' and I point at him in warning.

Another funny thing about Tramp: unlike many dogs, he doesn't just accept treats from everyone. If he doesn't like you, then you can go fuck yourself and keep your treat. So, of course, Ben is shite out of luck when he tries to bribe Tramp or make friends, or what the hell ever he thinks he's doing.

Ben ties Tramp up in the garden. Twice. Third time, Tramp enters the dining room Ben looks at me like I'm the one to blame.

"What the hell, Simon?" He whines and I just shrug.

"I didn't do anything." And I didn't tie the sodding bowline knot either! I stand up and snap my fingers at Tramp and he gladly follows me into the garden. There's a line tied to a garden table and groan loudly. I think I might give up on my sister and Ben, because what the hell, did they imagine would happen if Tramp was tied up to a table and he saw a squirrel? He wouldn't know the table is teak, he wouldn't know it was supposed to be heavy, he would just have taken off with the table bouncing behind him and doing more damage to the garden than an excavator out of control.

I grab the rope and tie it to the flagpole—with the cement foundation—instead. I then tie Tramp up with a bowline knot because Ben has carefully demonstrated it *several* times tonight. I pat Tramp on the head and then I walk away. I don't go far but turn around to look at Tramp. He's already bent his head and is nibbling the rope. I just stand there as Tramp somehow manages to untie the rope. It takes him a while, but he's patient and determined. I have no idea if it's blind luck, or if he knows what he's doing. Three times would suggest he does, and I absolutely can't wrap my head around that. It scares the living hell out of me.

"Are you shitting me?" I exclaim, just as he frees himself of the rope, stands up, and shakes himself.

Surprise.

"Did you just untie the rope?"

Tapping paws.

"That's bad, Tramp."

Whimpering.

So, it turned out if you don't tie the knot at the collar where he can't reach it with his teeth, he simply unties it, not giving a shite if it is a bowline knot. Told you my dog was smart.

Since then, Ben and Tramp have silently agreed to ignore each other. Tramp's promised Margot not to roam around the house and she has promised not to tie him up. He's allowed to guard their baby when Margot has given birth and in return, they're allowed to come near their own child.

Vetting

Fun fact: Husbands get upset if you fuck their wife.

We've got a new vet. I haven't met him yet, but we're heading there now. Our usual vet has asked us not to come back to her clinic. At the time, I thought she was perfectly fine being fucked in the storage room. She was, but her husband—and apparently her partner at the clinic—wasn't when he walked in on us. I took her doggy-style—very fitting for a vet—and I was very happy getting any. I was even succeeding in ignoring Tramp who was sprawled out on the floor like someone had just punctured him. Maybe the vet gave him a sedative when she administered the vaccine? Too bad I'm not fucking her on a regular basis, so I could've gotten some more of that miracle drug.

How does one end up fucking your dog's vet you may ask. Easily. We had been joking and flirting all the way through Tramp's check-up.

"He seems very calm," the vet said and stroked his back.

"He's a cockblocker," I grumbled.

"I can help you with that."

"Really?"

"Of course, I *am* a vet after all." She unbuttoned her labcoat and unhooked her bra at the front. That was not what I was imagining, but I'll take it! When an extremely busty woman puts her naked delights on full display and asks you through her lashes if you want to fuck her kind of pussy, you say you love all kinds of kind of animals. Truly.

We went to a storage room, she was naked except the lab-coat, I had only opened my jeans and rolled on a condom when she leaned over a pile of sacks with dry dog food. I flipped the lap-coat over her back, and she readily spread her legs for me so I could sink my cock deep into her from behind. I was happily pumping away when the door swung open and a man wearing another lab-coat entered.

"Jesus Christ, Alice!" He roared incensed.

"Get the fuck out," I growled.

"Stop fucking my wife."

"Your what?"

"Keep going," she urged and grabbed my naked ass with her hands. I had my hands on her ass, my cock in her pussy, and it was just all kinds of awkward. I don't fuck with an audience nearby and I don't fuck other men's wives or girlfriends.

"Christ, let go of me," I objected.

"Don't stop," she demanded and sunk her nails deep into my skin.

"What the hell, Alice?" The man yelled just as I pulled myself away from her and she straightened up.

"See that?" She said and pointed to my cock I hadn't even have time to shove back into my jeans—it can be a bit difficult with a hard-on.

"There's nothing to see," he said insulted. Both me and the vet snorted loudly.

"You're not as big as that!" She said rolling her eyes.

"Am too," he said defensively and let me tell you—he's not!

"It doesn't matter if you'd only use it."

"That's why you wanted that?" He asked and pointed towards me. He looked at my cock, the vet looked at my cock, Tramp looked at my cock.

"Stop discussing my cock," I roared, and I finally managed to button my jeans. Very painfully I might add.

"You get the hell out of here," the vet's husband growled as he advanced towards me. He didn't get far, and I didn't even get the chance to punch him, because Tramp stepped between us.

"What the hell?" I asked surprised. Tramp completely ignored me, because he was big puppy growling—very well indeed—and when the husband advanced further towards me Tramp's teeth clacked shut with a snapping sound only inches from the vet's groin. That made him stop instantly.

"Put that thing on a leash."

"You should do the same with your wife," I said, and Tramp looked pretty proud of *my* snarling. We didn't pay for that consultation—that's how I officially became a prostitute—and now we have a new vet.

There's something you've got to understand. When a guy usually has a very active sex-life, not having it…my guess it's like an alcoholic, who doesn't want to stop drinking. If he's forced to stop it means every time, he gets half a chance, he drinks. It doesn't matter what, or where, or when, because just about anything will do at this point. I wasn't embarrassed about fucking the vet in the storage room, because sadly, I've gotten used to having sex semi-public places, because it seems to be the only way for me these days. Not all people are comfortable around dogs—particularly not dogs the size of a small pony. Besides that, he is a cockblocker, so I rarely bring women home. I can't remember the last time I spent the night in a woman's bed either, because I've got my furry ball of chains at home.

I fucked Celia recently in the handicap toilet at the shopping centre. It was quite fortuitous I met her, and I was actually surprised she wanted to talk to me at all since Tramp ate her thong. Well, she didn't exactly want to *talk* to me. By miraculous timing, she had just broken up with her boyfriend—five minutes earlier—because he was unfaithful.

"Still not having much sex?" She asked.

"No."

"Still need it?"

"Hell, yeah."

"Make it good and make it quick." No problem. She yanked me into the handicap toilet and kissed me, and less than a minute later, her panties were pulled aside, she had her legs wrapped around my hips, I wore a condom, and I was fucking her against the wall. I successfully ignored when someone shouted and pounded on the door and fortunately it stopped—probably because Celia was moaning loudly. Seven minutes later, we were both done. We opened the door only to see a man in a wheelchair.

"Sorry about that," I said, but he wasn't listening to me. He was looking at Celia, who sauntered away in a criminally short skirt that barely covered her ass. If you looked closely enough, you could see wetness between her thighs. Knowing her, she might just be on her way to flaunt it in front of her ex.

"No problem," he said distractedly before he quickly wheeled himself into the bathroom. Not sure pissing was at the top of his mind anymore. I'm a bit sick of quickies to be honest, but at least I got to finish. This is the sad highlight of my sex-life for the past year. Very depressing.

*

Dogs smell. Even when they're not wet and farting, have rolled in something dead or equally disgusting. It's not necessarily a bad smell, but it's there and let me tell you…the larger the dog, the more it smells. Tramp smells even more than usual these days. He's been scratching his left ear so fiercely I've become worried about him taking his own head of when doing it. He's ground his ear against the floor with his bum in the air, looking ridiculous and he's been shaking his head so much I think he's shaken random brain cells lose. When I finally looked in his ear, I was almost floored by the stench. It smelled like something died in there, and that's why we're meeting the new vet today.

Tramp's not afraid of going to the vet. He hardly seems to register whenever he's injected or poked. He grunted and looked a bit 'what the fuck?' once when the vet shoved a finger up his bum—something about glands I *don't* want to know about. But in general, he doesn't care. I'm pretty happy about this, because honestly, I have no idea how I would get him in there if he refused. As it is, he trots into the waiting room with his head and tail held high like he's the king of the whole bloody place. Either that or a dressage horse. People are staring because he's a big fucker, and he's not quite two years yet. I've read somewhere that giant dogs are not fully grown until they're about three years old, which means he'll probably be growing for about another year. I have absolutely no idea how I'm going to deal with that.

It's clear when we enter the examination room, and I see the vet, there's no chance of us ending up fucking. He's a tiny man with small, round glasses, his hair looks like he's related to Einstein, and he has a slight hunch on his back. He looks at Tramp curiously.

"What do we have here?"

"It's a dog," I say, and the vet quirks one bushy eyebrow.

"I can see that. I *am* a vet you know?" He holds out his hand and I shake it. "Allan."

"Simon, and this is, Tramp."

"What breed is he?"

"No clue."

"Let's have a look," he says and gestures towards the examination table. I pat the table and Tramp jumps and puts his front legs on it, and then he's sort of stuck. I bend and lift his giant bum on the table, and he stands up. At this height, I can hardly see across Tramp's back and the vet adjusts the table. It's only two feet of the floor when he's happy about the height. Now, why the hell didn't he lower the table to begin with? Probably because he has a cousin who's a chiropractor and needs new clients—that's why.

The vet fearlessly grabs Tramp and shoves some kind of instrument into his ear. Tramp glances at him, then at me—like *I* have some kind of explanation for what's going on. I don't. Tramp gets uneasy and his snout twitches as the vet examines his ear. I gently pet his back. This seems to calm him, and I feel *very* important. Dogs can do that to you, and it feels really good. People like to feel important, and even the most useless wanker wants to be needed. I'm starting to believe that's why a lot of people have dogs.

"No mites," the vet says and the hairs on the back of my neck stand up.

"Mites?"

"Yes, that's pretty common."

"Really?" That sounds disgusting. The vet nods and keeps looking into Tramp's ear. There is a lot to look at.

"Aha," the vet says enthusiastically.

"Aha, what?" He doesn't answer but picks up one of those tweezer-looking scissors. Tramp cocks his head and glances at me like he wants me to tell him whatever the vet is doing to him is alright. I have absolutely no idea. I keep petting him and apparently that's all the comfort he needs. I can't very well tell Tramp I can't stand the smell and would rather have a semi-deaf dog who smells nicer, can I? He doesn't listen half the time anyway, so I'm wondering if I'll ever know the difference. Tramp grunts repeatedly as the vet digs in his ear.

"Aha!" The vet exclaims again like he's a detective who has just uncovered an important clue to solving a murder. I won't be surprised if he actually has, because that ear smells pretty much like there is a rotting corpse in there. He triumphantly holds up…I don't know what the hell that is. It kind of looks like pellet—only Tramp's not a bird, and that's his ear—not his mouth. But with him everything is possible I suppose.

"What is that?" I ask.

"I have no idea," the vet says enthusiastically. "Can I keep it?"

"Please do," I say disgusted.

"It looks like there's a bit of dirt and grass in there and is that…orange marmalade?"

"Probably."

"Really?"

"Nothing surprises me anymore."

"Hmm," the vet says before he pours some kind of liquid into Tramp's ear. Tramp looks like he's just had a brain freeze, but it turns into weird grunting as the vet massages his ear. It sounds rather squishy and that's got to make one hell of a lot of noise inside Tramp's head. When the vet stops massaging his ear Tramp looks dizzy—or maybe a bit horny. Wouldn't be surprised by that one.

"Is it supposed to sound like that?" I ask and the vet nods.

"Oh, yes, quite normal."

"Well, that's a first."

"Can he shake his head at command?" The vet asks, and I groan. I knew I should *not* have worn clean clothes today. I look at Tramp.

"If you shake your head right now, you're going to make a real big mess," I tell him seriously.

"Simon, I don't think…" The vet doesn't even get to finish his sentence before Tramp shakes his heads like he's going for a self-inflicted concussion. Ear-cleaner, and what the hell ever has been dislodged from Tramp's brain, sprays every corner of the room like somebody switched on a dirty sprinkler. The vet naively holds out his hands to shield himself, but I just stand there and take it. Round two as well. "Wow," the vet says as he pokes his head out from behind a small cupboard where he's taken cover.

"Like that?" I ask drily.

"That was actually rather impressive," he says and looks around the room. I'm pretty sure I'm going to pay for additional cleaning of the examination room. Like I said: everything concerning Tramp costs money.

The vet wipes Tramp's ear and I let Tramp jump—or rather step—of the table.

"He's a funny-looking thing, isn't he?" The vet says as he rubs Tramps sides.

"That's one way of putting it."

"There's got to be a lot of different breads here."

"Like what?"

"Size could indicate Great Dane, the ears too. Fur looks a bit like an Irish Wolfhound. He's heavier though. Is he a runner?"

"You have no idea," I say drily.

"Fetches?" I nod.

"I think he does pretty much of everything."

"I can well believe it."

"Any chance he may be part cat?"

"Ah, no Simon, that's not how it works. Why?"

"He's an asshole." The vet blinks.

"Oh, a cat joke," he deadpans and nods understandingly. Guess that wasn't funny.

"He howls and talks like this crazy Husky I've seen on YouTube."

"That could also be German Shepard," he says and nods towards Tramp's tail which could look like a slightly scruffy German Shepard tail.

"Or just a really annoying personality," I mumble.

Scowl and promise of endless howling.

The vet pulls Tramp's lips back and looks at his teeth.

"Good boy," he praises as Tramp lets him pull his lips and chin and I roll my eyes. He's not a good boy—this is only a temporary act. I don't tell the vet I've practiced looking at Tramp's teeth because I was certain I'd be retrieving something living from them at some point. But it comes in pretty handy at the vet too.

"He looks good, Simon."

Proud look.

"You mean healthy?" I ask for clarification.

Scowl.

"Yes, yes, very healthy," the vet says, and he's still looking at Tramp curiously. "You could buy a DNA-test if you want to know for certain." See…everything costs money.

"It's not going to change anything," I say with a shrug. My money is on the vet will end up being so curious he might do it for free one day. Tramp is spending my money on more essential things at the moment. The vet looks disappointed. If it's because I won't pay to satisfy his curiosity or because he doesn't sell me the DNA-test, I don't know.

"So, maybe you are part German Shepard," I tell Tramp when we leave the vet.

Glance and huff. Clearly not impressed.

"My money's on the Husky with all the noise you're making."

Stops and lifts leg to demonstratively pee on a perfectly innocent bush.

"You're far noisier."

Lifts tail.

"You're happy about that?"

Tail wagging.

"You would be, wouldn't you?"

Smirk.

I put the plastic bag with the ear cleaner in the front seat. Even if I bought the one with the most boring packaging—blue and white, medical-looking, no aloe vera—I'm not leaving it with Tramp. No way. I open the boot, and he readily jumps into the cage I've gotten for him. It was expensive like hell—too—but it definitely makes sense. Tramp roaming free can in general be questionable, Tramp roaming freely in a car is a recipe for an accident of epic proportions. As I start the car, the radio comes on and eighties duet with Madonna and Prince blasts out, and Tramp promptly starts howling like he's slowly being tortured to death before I even have time to change the channel. I hate that song too, but really?

There's this guy…Swashbuckling rogue, not bad with the ladies, either. Not that he would brag about it, of course. He wears aviator sunglasses, military-looking sports-watch, and often Timberland boots. His firm ass and long legs are on display in worn blue jeans and his pecs is showing under a black T-shirt. He's six-foot-four, muscular, about two-hundred ten pounds, blue eyes. His hair is dark brown, and he often looks like he just rolled out of bed, including the five o'clock shadow. He's fit, he's attractive, his friends tease him and call him a walking, talking jeans commercial. Women like his ass, they pinch it when he goes out, they like to look at him. They *love* the size of his cock, they like to flirt and rub against him when they dance with him, and he's gotten laid plenty. He doesn't back down in a barfight, and he can hold his own—mostly. All in all, he's pretty cool. He drives a black Range Rover. The window is often rolled down and he's casually leaning his elbow at the door. He looks cool, and if you ever meet him in traffic…don't forget about all this when you hear his taste in music. Please don't judge. Maybe he isn't listening to 'Girls Just Want to Have Fun' with Cyndi Lauper or 'Blue' with Eiffel 65 or Bee Gees falsetto because he likes it. Maybe he listens to it because his asshole dog loves it—and any other music sounding like a singing chipmunk. I actually like Cyndi, but not on repeat for fifteen minutes because it pleases Tramp when we're stuck in traffic.

*

Once I had the latest and most expensive smartphone. I don't anymore. I had it for about two days. That's probably the only time I've been so furious at Tramp, I was tempted to punch him for real. Didn't do it though. I'm not a rich guy and Tramp's a walking, barking savings killer even when he doesn't eat anything he's not supposed to.

Do you know the old spaghetti-western 'The Good, the Bad and the Ugly' from 1966? It's epic! It was directed by Sergio Leone and starred Clint Eastwood, Lee Van Cleef and Eli Wallach. You know the main theme too? You must because it's legendary. It's by Ennio Morricone and it's the best *ever*. It even surpasses the theme from 'Jaws' by John Williams in my book. That movie is from 1975 by the way. But naturally I had 'The Good, the Bad and the Ugly' for a ringtone on my brand, new phone. Yes, you heard me...*had*. The tune made Tramp go ballistic for some reason. One day, when I was in the shower, I heard my phone ringing in the living room. Until suddenly, I didn't hear it anymore. The theme from 'Jaws' was suddenly creeping into my head, and I sprinted out the shower and into the living room, where I found the victim who clearly was no more. For gory details regarding the remains please see the 'Jaws' book by Peter Benchley from 1974. This was equally grim.

Tramp had chewed it to pieces and one of his canines had almost bitten all the way through the phone. I called the vet—on my old phone—and he said as long, as Tramp only chewed it, he should be all right. This really surprised me, because I thought my vet would love any reason to see Tramp and bill me for nothing. I did hear some insane meowing in the background though, so maybe that's why the vet was willing to gamble Tramp's life. At that moment I was too.

I grabbed Tramp's collar and looked him dead in the eyes until he looked away and I ignored him for the rest of the day. I sent him to his ridiculously large and expensive orthopaedic bed, and I've got to say that's the only time Tramp has been this quiet for such a long time. Our walk in the park was brief and only with the leash on. In the evening, he was shuffling to me with his tail between his legs in a nervous wagging. When I looked at him, he started crawling towards me on his stomach and when he reached me, he lay down in front of me and rolled onto his back. And then I felt *so* guilty. I felt I had to sit on the floor and pet him for hours and apologise for being mad at him, because *he* did something wrong. Dogs can do that to you. No wonder, dog owners are crazy.

Not Bloody Pongo

Fun fact: The dog (Canis familiaris or Canis lupus familiaris) is a domesticated form of wolf. The dog descends from an ancient, extinct wolf, with the modern wolf being the dog's nearest living relative. And according to a thousand memes, they regret daily that they ever approached humans.

For some reason, Tramp's got a new routine. He thinks five in the morning is a bloody excellent time to wake up. I'd probably think so too if I knew I could nap a dozen times during the day. If I didn't have to work, could fuck a unicorn, and if I could lick my own balls. I think I'd make a pretty happy dog. A man can dream.

I've given up on ignoring him in the morning. For one thing, I swear I can feel him staring at me, even when I'm sleeping. Another thing is, he simply pulls the blanket and the duvet of me. I've considered holding on to it, but the thought of the duvet ripping and filling the room with feathers is enough for me to get my ass and morning wood out of bed. Told you he's an asshole.

Every bloody morning, I leave my shredded dignity in the apartment and walk out the door in boots, jacket, pj bottoms and occasionally a T-shirt. My hair's a joke, I drag my feet, and my balls are freezing off because I don't wear underwear when I can avoid it, and let's face it—pj bottoms are not the least bit outdoorsy. My body is not awake yet, so it doesn't take into consideration it's June and it's probably a nice summer morning—I'm still cold.

Today, I see a lone female runner is running along the lake, and she immediately catches Tramp's attention. He pulls the leash and I feel so smart because I haven't taken it of him yet. He keeps pulling until I yank it.

"No."

Desperate whine.

"She's not even your species and you're not bloody Pongo at matchmaking, you know?"

Scowl.

"I had no problem picking up women on my own until you came along."

Blank stare like he understands absolutely nothing of what I'm saying—pretty plausible that one—and then he turns to look at the woman running.

"Don't even think about it."

Quiet whimpering. Tapdancing on the spot.

Chances are I've got about three seconds before he takes off and if I'm not paying attention, he can surprise me and pull me on my ass. Speaking of ass, that's a fucking amazing ass on the woman running. I need to get laid. Bad.

Tramp's a couch potato and doesn't move much during the day, so how the hell he manages to have muscles and explosive force like Superman taking off against the stratosphere is beyond me. The guy's a slob. If I were a slob like that, I'd look like Jabba the Hutt, have absolutely no superpowers, and I wouldn't even make it out the front door—much less the stratosphere.

Tramp lets out an exited bark and I tense every muscle in my body just in time as he lunges forward—or at least tries to. He falls on his ass when I yank the leash hard.

"No," I growl, and he looks confused like he doesn't understand what the hell just happened, even if I've done this about a hundred times already. Sometimes, he's so stupid, sometimes, I think he's contemplating building a rocket to escape my evil regime.

The woman turns her head at his bark and...shite...it's the angry one I've flashed most of my ass. Strangely, she heads our way and looks at me happily—or maybe it's Tramp she's smiling at.

"I'm not calling you a tramp today *either*," I say defensively as soon as she gets close enough to hear, but she ignores me. Her smile was definitely for Tramp.

"Hey, Tramp," she coos as she holds out to back of her hand for him to sniff. Only he doesn't sniff, he enthusiastically licks her hand. He's wagging his tale—and most of his body—in excitement, and I tense up, so he doesn't yank my arm loose at the socket. Judging by his enthusiasm his lipstick dick comes out in a moment—I'm not taking responsibility for that one. "Hey, gorgeous," she says as Tramp throws himself at her feet. She squats and bends over so she can rub his chest.

"He's pretty happy to see you," I say as I try to ignore the completely amazing view I have of her tits in the sports bra when she's leaning over.

"I like you, don't I boy?" She says this to Tramp who looks like he just died and gone to heaven and there's an angel petting him. If angels look even half as sexy as this one, I'm killing myself when we get home. Tramp, have fun in the apartment—you're on your own.

"So, it's *dogs* you like."

"Still wearing practically nothing, I see."

"You don't have to check out my cock every time you see me, you know?"

"Hard not to."

"Not hard yet, but I'll get there."

"Not waiting around for that."

"Your loss."

"Nice to see you, Tramp," she says and looks at him. Not me.

Whenever Tramp is being petted, he shoves you with his paws like he's playing hard to get—even if he's as cheap, as a hungry whore, when it comes to being petted by people he likes. So, it's no surprise when the angry woman bends to straighten the tights Tramp has pushed up her leg. Jesus, that's one gorgeous ass. As she turns and leaves, her top has hitched up, and I see a tattoo on her lower back. Tramp whines like he's seen it too and wants to lick it—I know I certainly do.

"No, Tramp, a tramp stamp doesn't mean she's your property," I tell him, forgetting we're not alone. The woman stiffens and stops and then she slowly turns towards me. Oh shite. Tramp whimpers.

"What did you just say?"

"What's written on your back?" I say in an attempt, to be casual—and ignore what I just said.

"Please fuck me harder."

"I'd be up for that." I say before I can help myself. Tramp lets out another small whimper beside me, and I don't blame him, because that was a fucking dumb thing to say. He might also whimper out of fear because that's one pissed woman looking at me. Her eyes are on fire, and I think I might be able to outrun even Tramp to escape her right now. But damn, she's sexy when she's angry. Like I said—I really need to get laid.

"I can't believe how big of an asshole you are!" she snarls. I don't say anything…I've got nothing. At least she doesn't punch me before she turns and runs away. Jesus, that's one sexy ass.

*

Tramp's birthday is in a few days—I haven't told him though—and I'm still not certain there's any reason to celebrate. And I'm not yet so dog owner crazy I'm getting him a cake and hosting a party. I'm not singing for him either and I'm definitely not making him wear a paper hat like the suffering dogs on memes. Besides, he doesn't deserve a party—he really doesn't.

He steps on my toes every chance he gets, he's expensive, he won't let me sleep, he's a cockblocker, the sexy, running woman likes him better than me, his farts smell horrible, he drags me to the park constantly, and shakes himself off *right* in front of me when he's wet. He also sabotages every attempt I've made for entertaining him. I got him a slow feed dog bowl because it was supposed to be good for him not eating his food like I am starving him to death. He looked at the bowl, licked into the gaps a few times, then he grabbed the edge of the bowl, and flipped it upside down. The dry food was all over the floor and Tramp wolfed it down as fast as he usually does. He's not the only dog to do this at all, and that's why

I'm asking you: how the hell does the pet industry make us believe the shite they come up with time and time again? I have no clue. I went to the pet shop and asked the boy for my money back by sheer principle. But since Tramp left his teeth marks on the side, they claimed it was non-refundable. The pet industry—and Tramp—won again.

On Tramp's birthday—I still don't tell him—I'm feeling generous, and I take him to the dog park. He's happy and if he complains I swear to God, I'll buy him a paper hat and make a meme out of him.

Among the dog owners in the dog park, I like Axel and Kent. Probably, *only* Axel and Kent. I met them one day when I was fairly new to the dog park. I was standing by myself, and they were kind enough to approach me. After an introduction they pointed towards a group of *owners*—that's right, here we are not people or humans, here we are merely owners—no doubt attempting to include me.

"They don't like me," I said dismissively.

"Okay, what about them?" Kent said and pointed towards the woman, who has once refused that her dog will eat a couch if it gets hungry enough, was standing with a few others.

"They don't like me either," I admitted.

"And them?" Axel said and pointed towards the man whose dog would have died in the Middle Ages.

"Let's just assume for the moment that everyone here doesn't like me," I said tiredly. Axel giggled and patted my arm.

"Don't worry, love. We like you."

Axel and Kent have two tan—don't you *dare* call it light brown—American Cocker Spaniels, which are always groomed to perfection. Kent is a professional hairdresser, and it shows on the dogs. They're gay and with their groomed dogs they are so stereotypical it's almost not funny. Almost. But I really like them, and I often stick to them when I'm at the park. Of course, they are dog owner crazy, but they hide it pretty well. I think their dogs are called Darling—both of them—because whenever they call for them it's 'Darlings' with the enthusiasm of a pre-school teacher who pretends the building's not on fire and the evacuation is merely another super fun school trip.

"Did you meet the new one?" Axel asks and rolls his eyes.

"The new what?"

"Owner."

"She's a snob," Kent says looking very offended—and utterly feminine.

"And here she comes," Axel whispers just as a blonde woman walks over to us in a pace that indicates ambitious and pretentious dog owner. They are the *worst*.

"I'm Judith," she says and holds out her hand.

"Simon," I say and try not to wince as she crunches my hand like she's wrinkling divorce papers. She has probably done that too. She quickly looks me up and down—including my groin—and glances briefly at Axel and Kent.

"I haven't seen you around," she says and cocks her head, no doubt trying to decide if I'm with Kent and Axel or just holding both of them hostage in a dungeon for my dirty pleasure. I already don't like her—I'm not even tempted to fuck her—so, I'm not going to encourage any kind of conversation. I don't like fanatics.

"Sorry, blondie, I don't do back-story," I say with a shrug. "So, which one is yours?" I ask and nod towards the flock of dogs running around playing and sniffing and doing doggy things. I don't give a shite, I really don't, but I've learned it's what you ask other *owners*.

"You know Game of Thrones?" She asks me disdainfully.

"And here we go," Kent mumbles under his breath.

"Yeah," I say, because of course I do, I'm not an amateur. I've even read the books.

"*My* dog is the one who looks like a dire wolf." Oh, so that's where this was going. I just shrug.

"My dog makes a dire wolf look like a pussy," I snort. Do you hear me dog owner bragging? I'm getting *so* good at this. Axel and Kent chuckles beside me.

"Really?" She huffs arrogantly. "Mine is a Tamaskan." I have no idea what the hell that is.

"Mine's an accident."

"Mine's really rare," she says angrily.

"Mine's one of a kind." She's obviously run out of arguments, so she looks me up and down and then scoffs at me like she now finds me lacking in every way. Which—I might add—is not possible. She lets out a series of whistles that sounds almost like an entire composition, and I think even Roger Whitaker would be envious. A moment later, a dog comes running. My money's on it couldn't stand the noise this woman is emitting and it's smart enough to know she'll go on forever if it doesn't obey her.

The dog has light brown and white fur and I've got to say it looks pretty much like 'Summer.' It's cute, it looks like a wolf, but it's only about twenty-four inches. Poor thing. I pet the wannabe dire wolf and it seems to enjoy it. Not sure the pompous owner does. In general, dogs like me—for some unknown reason—and Tramp allows me to pet them for a limited amount of time. However, he *won't* allow me to say something nice to them—that's for him only once in a while. Guess he likes me after all.

"So, which one is yours?" She asks disdainfully—again—like the presence of her dog proves her point. I'm not impressed.

"The special one," I say, knowing full well she won't like it.

"*Mine* is the special one," she insists furiously. Both Axel and Kent snicker. I stop petting the dog and straighten up—because apparently, you have to bend to pet a pussy dire wolf. I let out a short, loud whistle—Matt taught me—and moments later, Tramp comes running. Might have something to do with the reward he's expecting, but I'm still pleased. He bumps slightly into me as he rounds me and sits down. I reward him anyway, since I have no idea how the hell, I'm going to teach him *not* to bump into me.

"That's not a dog," the pussy dire wolf owner exclaims. She sounds almost horrified.

Incensed look.

"Yes, he is."

"It's not," she insists.

Roll of eyes.

"What do you think it is then?" I ask. She blinks and looks at Tramp and looks at me.

"I have absolutely no idea," she says slowly.

"He's a dog," I say. I can't believe I'm having this conversation.

"It's a mongrel."

Whimper.

"So? The definition of mongrel is a *dog* of no definable type or breed." I've looked it up—yes, really.

"It's a monster," she says.

"At least he's not a pussy," I say with a smirk and look at her fancy dire wolf-looking dog which has just rolled on its back and is letting Tramp stiff her…I'm tempted to call it pussy, but a pussy on a dog doesn't quite sound right, does it? In a moment, he'll start licking her, and then he'll have had more oral sex than I've had for ages. That's so depressing. I think the same thought crosses the angry woman's mind, because she lets out a gasp of horror.

"Jasmine," she shrieks and the pussy dire wolf jerks and stands up abruptly. It doesn't look happy about the interruption and, believe me, I know the feeling. The angry owner and her fancy dog quickly walk away from us. At least she didn't punch me.

"Are you shitting me?" I ask.

"About the woman, the whistling, or the name of the dog?" Axel asks.

"All three I think."

"Unfortunately, not."

Whimpering.

"Don't mind her, Tramp," Axel says and pats him comfortingly. I don't think that's why he's whimpering, but what do I know? "She was just an evil woman, who doesn't appreciate you."

"I can do your fur," Kent offers Tramp.

Whining and a pleading look.

"Really?" I ask with a smug look towards Tramp.

Panic.

"Absolutely," Kent says enthusiastically. I glance at Tramp who looks very much like a deer caught in the headlights, and it's not only because of his size. I look at

Tramp and I just barely manage to tamper down what I'm sure would be a villain-worthy grin. Kind of like Willem Dafoe in Spiderman when Norman Osborne has a melt down and The Green Goblin surfaces. That movie is from 2002, and as far as movie villain insanity goes, Dafoe's performance is yet to be surpassed.

About Ten Square Feet

Fun fact: When a really big dog has diarrhoea, it takes up about ten square feet of the floor.

It's Tuesday, I've only just come home and when I open the door to my apartment, I'm immediately worried, because Tramp is not here to greet me. If you ever need an ego-boost, if you ever want to feel needed and wanted and popular—get a dog. Seriously. The worry is quickly overcome by the foul smell filling the air. Tramp comes shuffling into the hallway from the living room, he's looking miserable, and his tail is carefully wagging between his legs.

The stench is unbelievable, and I push past him and look into the living room. There's some kind of brown substance all over the floor. There're…lumps in there, and something that looks like…slime too. I look towards Tramp who's now on his ridiculously large and expensive orthopaedic bed and he's looking so ashamed I can't even be pissed at him, even when my stomach heaves and I rush to the bathroom.

Rubber gloves on, and desperately wishing I had a biohazard suit and mask, I get to work cleaning up. I've stripped down to nothing because I think I might have a panic attack if I get even a single speck of liquid shite on my clothes. Yes, honestly. I've let Tramp into the bathroom—it'll be easier to wash if he's not finished emitting his chemical experiment. The stench is unbelievable. I try not to breathe through my nose, but when I breathe through my mouth, I almost feel like I can taste it. Not a good idea either. I should've practiced holding my breath for occasions just like this. Why haven't I thought of that?

I use three rolls of paper towels and eight plastic bags before I'm done. I wear a random scarf from the coat rack to cover my cock and half my ass when I drop them down the garbage chute in the hallway. I am very happy I meet none of the other residents, but I wouldn't put it past my neighbour across the hall to just stay still on the other side of the door and jerk off to the sight of my improvised miniskirt. His name is Samuel, he's a tiny man, he has a pointed nose, and he looks like a rodent. He turned thirty last year, but he still has spots like a teenager. He's pale and blond and have an overall sickly air about him. He's also gay, which seems to be the only normal thing about him. I'm not homophobic, honestly, but when he first moved in, he approached me several times and asked me if I by any chance was gay, I got really creeped out. When I said no, he asked me if I'd consider it. When I said no to that, he asked me if he could fuck me anyway. When I said no to that too, he asked me if he could watch the next time, I fucked a woman. When I said no to that he asked if he could see me naked. You see where this is going right? When I declined everything, he asked me, he seemed to give up and I was pretty disgusted. I thought we'd gotten that out of the way, but the next day there was a post-it on my front door "Hey Baby, come over anytime, you want to play. Love Sammy." I let Tramp eat the note and I even praised him for it—

particularly because Samuel had also drawn something that looked an awful lot like handcuffs. Shiver.

I hear loud whimper from the bathroom, and I stop dead in my tracks. The wood floor cleaner is begging me from the dining room table, but the thought of cleaning up any more shite quickly decides for me. I frantically pull on my jeans and shove my feet into my boots. I grab the leash and go to the bathroom. Thank God, it smells like it usually does. Tramp's stomach rumbles and then I panic. Completely. I pull him out the bathroom and to the apartment door. I snatch my keys, put the leash on him, and run out the door. Tramp is looking strained and if he shites on the stairs I think I might kill myself.

We make it down the stairs and we pass Mr Roberts by the entrance door.

"Simon, you're not dressed," he calls out after me, but I ignore him and sprint towards the park like a maniac, while I'm practically dragging Tramp behind me.

"Ugh! Come on, fleabag, forward!" I yell. The park is about half a mile away and with the pace I'm setting I'm probably going to collapse before we even get there, but I don't care. Tramp's barely keeping up and that worries me because usually he can outrun me like I'm a tortoise.

I'm only wearing jeans and boots and I'm breathing hard from my frantic sprint when we get to the park. Tramp looks pained like he's about to shite himself to death and standing down-wind from him it almost smells like he did die a while ago. My stomachs heaves, but I've got nothing left to give. I just stand there with my hands on my knees for support and feel miserable while I throw up a few drops of stomach acid while I struggle to breathe.

In case you'd like to know: in situations like this, you don't answer a four-year-old boy when he's asking what your dog is doing. If you're tempted to do so anyway you don't say 'shitting himself to death.' Not unless you want to be threatened by his uptight mother at least. She does *not* appreciate honesty, almost nakedness, and the stench of rotten shite. Can't really blame her on that last part, but I still wonder what kind of man would ever fuck her—much less get her pregnant. It seems like a really bad idea. Even in my present abstinent state I wouldn't fuck her, and that's really saying something.

And just in case you'd also like to know: you can't pick up diarrhoea with a poop bag.

Despite Tramp's miserable appearance, the wind and darkening sky, and my lack of clothing, I decide we're going for a walk. A very, very long one. I need to make absolutely certain he's emptied his stomach and intestines—preferably forever. We've barely made it round the pond when two police officers on horseback approach and you know that gut feeling? Right now, I just know its's me they're looking for.

The police officers are two women and for a moment my sex-deprived brain wonder if they will ride something human instead. Deprived, depraved—it's almost the same. Feels like it to me at least. One of the horses bends its head towards Tramp and Tramp steps close to greet, sniff…I don't know what the hell they're doing. Maybe the horse thinks it's gotten a new pony friend. I'm a bit wary of horses. To me they're like a twelve-hundred-pound neurosis and my mind is already making up scenarios of a panicked, prancing horse and me getting hurt. There's no doubt in my mind Tramp is not the one who will get trampled on.

One officer dismount, and she looks surprised to see me. "Simon?"

"Hey, Laura," I say surprised because I know her. Sort of. Well, at least I remember having sex with her. It's mostly because she wore those strange boots that looked like she kicked a teddy bear so hard her feet got stuck up its ass. She took them off in bed, but still, that's the most memorable thing about her. In case you are wondering…yes, she rides humans as well.

I make a clicking sound with my mouth and Tramp sits down, even if I think I see him wince, as his bum hits the gravel. Some people use that clicking sound with horses, but since Tramp is as big as a pony, I think it's very fitting. Both horses look at me, but fortunately they don't move.

"We got a report from a distressed woman of a half-naked confused man wandering in the park telling children obscenities. I expected the usual disgusting old flasher, I didn't think it'd be you."

"Neither did I." She giggles and that's another thing I suddenly remember about her. It's a truly annoying sound and that's how we ended up roleplaying 'burglar gags woman' when I fucked her. She loved it. I'm not sure I did.

"You still look hot as hell," she says as her eyes wander over my bare upper body and besides the chill, I suddenly have another reason for wishing I brought a jacket. It's not the temperature that's responsible for the goosebumps spreading all over my body. "Very fuckable." She's wearing a yellow jacket, helmet, black trousers, and a lot of gadgets—I'd be lying if I said she looked fuckable too.

"Still married?" I ask instead.

"Still married, but if you..." I shake my head. I don't fuck other people's wives—especially not when all I remember about her is that she kicked a teddy bear's ass, and her giggling is annoying. Besides, if she liked being gagged, I shudder at the thought of what she wants to do with the gun and handcuffs she's got strapped to her belt. Tramp is getting uneasy beside me, and I just hope he'll keep calm while Laura is here.

"You know I don't do that," I say. Not intentionally at least.

"I could fine you for not being dressed and distressing other people, you know."

"I know," I say evenly.

"I might not if you reconsider."

"My prostitution days are behind me," I declare.

"Really?" She cocks an eyebrow like she doesn't believe a word I'm saying.

"Really."

"You want the fine instead?"

"You'll have one hell of a hassle making it stick when I complain about it. It's not like I'm flashing my ass or swinging my cock around."

"Would you like to? In private?"

"I'd rather not."

"What happened to you?" She asks, looking very surprised.

"I got a dog," I say and gently pat Tramp's head. It's not difficult considering his head is almost at my waist when he's sitting down. Laura eyes Tramp dubiously.

"You should probably stay clear of other people today," she finally says, and I nod.

"Gladly." Because that means I should stay clear of her too. I turn and walk away, and Tramp looks very relieved to stand up again. Pain in the ass has so many meanings right now.

"That one used to be the best fuck in the city," Laura says quietly to the other officer like she can't believe what's happened to me. I can't believe it either.

"Use your cuffs, find out if he still is." They giggle and I pretend I don't hear them as shivers run up my spine. When it starts to rain my life is complete.

"I'm not feeding you ever again," I tell Tramp as we slowly walk down the path. I attempt to ignore I'm freezing—at least it's not my balls this time—and the weird looks people are giving me. But I need to make absolutely certain Tramp's done before I bring him anywhere near home again. He cowers and looks desolate—making me feel guilty immediately. Dogs can do that to you.

"I didn't mean it," I say softly.

Ears perk slightly.

"I'm just trying to take care of you."

Humble wagging of tail between his legs.

"You must feel like shite."

Whine.

"Sorry, bad joke."

Pleading look.

"Maybe we should get you some oatmeal or something."

Whimper.

"Yoghurt…" I ponder. "Chicken."

Tail not standing, but at least not between his legs.

"Cottage cheese."

Bark.

Great. My dog likes the sound of the word 'cottage cheese.' He'll regret it.

He doesn't regret it, and he eats a massive meal consisting of a nasty-looking mix of boiled to death chicken and cottage cheese. Maybe he's blind and have no tastebuds? That would at least explain him eating the lavender scented candles. When he burps delighted, I cross my fingers that I won't regret feeding him. I might kill myself if he shites all over the place again. Yes, really.

For once, I'm happy I had to rearrange my entire life when I got Tramp. My apartment is seven-hundred-fifty square feet and with a large canine of indeterminable breed that's not much. When I got Tramp, I sorted my furniture and only kept the most essential—I call it 'forced minimalism.' He needed the space and I needed not to get my home ruined. Even unintentionally Tramp ruined a lot of things as he grew. His tail alone is responsible for the mass destruction of every plant, every candlestick, and every other knick-knack my mother thought I needed at some point. Now, I have the best excuse for not having any and not accepting any for a long, long time. I hate knick-knack and if my mother presents me with more ever again, I can get rid of it, and claim Tramp's tail has killed it. Perfect.

Also, I need the floor for training. You don't ask a dog his size to roll over unless you've cleared a lot of space. He doesn't care whether there's a speaker, or a lamp, or a small table in his way—he rolls anyway and is totally unaffected when he ruins something. Sometimes, the noise of things breaking startles him, but most of the time, he doesn't care at all. When he barged into the side table and it got stuck around his neck, he looked confused, then resigned, and then he ignored it. I considered taking him to the park like that, but in the end, I decided against it. Knowing dog owners, I'd probably be attacked and beaten because I tortured my dog even worse than when I feed him regular dog food. I did, however, snap several pictures of him wearing the table. It was bloody hilarious.

Few furniture also means Tramp didn't hit anything besides the floor when he made his shitshow earlier, and I'm very happy about that. The apartment doesn't smell of shite when we get home, because I opened the door to the Juliet balcony—that's a very good thing. The rain has poured into the living room because the door was left open—that's a really bad thing. There's usually a downside to everything that has to do with Tramp and tonight is no exception. There's a large puddle on the floor, the couch is wet, and there's an aquarium in the making in my magazine holder. This evening has already lasted forever, you know with the shite and Laura, walking around in the rain, drying both of us when we got home, and making Tramp his alternative dinner. Now, I need to wipe the floor, empty the magazine holder, and lay everything in it out to dry. This is not the best night of my life I'll tell you that.

*

I'm still practicing being a dog owner and I think Tramp's practicing his own abilities. One night, when I was playing with him and crawling on the floor, he opened his mouth over my head like he was testing if it would fit—it did. If he decides to bite something for real someday whatever it is…is no more. As Tramp keeps growing, so does my responsibility.

I even bought a dog behaviour book one day—which Tramp shredded the next day when he was home alone. Proves my point.

Everything concerning a dog cost either money or time. The walks, the training, the tricks, the attention. And then, there's the money. New car—still slightly bitter about that—food, toys, miscellaneous victims, and then there's the vet's cash register that happens to say ka-ching every time I enter the clinic. Maybe it's just coincidence.

I've tried involving Tramp and giving him chores to do. I've taught him to bring the unicorn to the washer—so far, I haven't been able to stop him from staring at the washer for the entire hour it takes to wash his pet. I know a lot of dogs do this—I just hoped Tramp was smarter. But at least I know where to find him.

I've tried to teach him a lot of things, hoping to keep him too busy or too tired to eat the wall or figure out he has a really good shot at eating the front door to escape. He's pretty good at 'fetch' and 'bring' and 'find' and 'let go.' He can also carry things besides the unicorn, but of course, he gets bored halfway up the stairs, and drops whatever he's carrying. We're practicing 'careful' and for my own amusement, I've practiced 'still' meaning he has to sit still, so I can balance something at his massive snout. I take a lot of pictures of that. I need to teach him to bob his head and catapult the treat into the air and catch it. That trick is only useful for entertaining his owner, but I think it's very important.

And here's a lesson for you: don't teach your dog things you don't want it to do. Don't let other people teach *your* dog tricks, *you* don't want it to actually do. I don't have to tell you that has already happened, don't I? The culprit is my father.

That's right, my own flesh and blood and the man who told me I was an idiot for taking the dog. There's a lot of funny memes about people who didn't want dogs but now they can't do without them. My father is smarter than that—somehow—because he doesn't keep Tramp, he just entertains him and consequently fucks things up for me. He's done it by letting Tramp help him in the garden. Helping meaning digging. Bad idea. I'm telling you, bad fucking idea. So, now Tramp knows the command 'dig' too, and his huge paws and claws makes him just about as efficient as an excavator on power fuel. Thanks, Dad.

Thanks to the pet industry, I've brought home an activity treat ball. Tramp looks very interested as I fill it with treats, and I cross my fingers it'll keep him entertained for a while. But whatever kinds of dogs Tramp is, he's not stupid—at least not today. He pushes the ball around with his snout and then a treat falls out. He does it again—nothing happens. And again, and another treat. He stares at the ball and then he lays down on the floor. He lays his paw on the ball and tilts it from left to right gradually making the treats fall out almost like an automatic feeding machine. It takes him about three minutes to empty the whole fucking thing. When he's done, he licks his nose and looks at me like he's saying, 'what are we doing now?' I want to kill myself—and I'll be looking for a more difficult one in support of the greedy pet industry.

A part of Tramp's training is also being left outside shops. Usually, it's only the coffee shop because I can discreetly keep an eye on him. So far, it hasn't been necessary for me to rush out of the shop and save anything—I'm very happy about that. But today might prove an exception.

Three teenage boys are standing close by and they're clearly talking about Tramp, because they're smiling and pointing in the holy shite-kind of way. He gets that a lot. Fortunately, he's not bothered by it and is still sniffing the lamp post I've tied him to. You don't tie a dog his size to anything that's not either metal and cast firmly in the ground, or an oak tree that's at least a hundred years old. Trust me on this.

I pay for my coffee and cookie and I'm almost out the door when one of the teenage boys jumps towards Tramp.

"Booh!" He shouts loudly and Tramp jerks in sheer surprise. It takes him about half a second to recover and then his hackles rise like someone pushed a button. He lets out a dangerous-sounding snarl, his lips are pulled back, and all his teeth are shoving. Jaws, swim home. All three teenagers tumble back in fear, and I grab the one who frightened Tramp by the collar of his jacket. He's a tall kid, about six-foot-six, but he's gangly and I've got weight and a lot of muscle on him.

"Are you trying to get yourself killed?" I ask calmly, but loud enough to be heard over Tramps snarling.

"No, sir," he stutters as I cock an eyebrow and look at him. Sir? Fuck, I'm getting old. Or maybe I just look it—I blame Tramp.

"Then what the fuck were you doing?" I make a clicking sound with my mouth and Tramp slams his bum down the pavement. Fuck, I'm so proud right now.

"Nothing, sir."

"Really?" I ask. "To me it looked like you were being fucking stupid." I let go of his collar and he almost slumps to the pavement.

"I'm sorry, sir," he says.

"Not as sorry as you'd have been if he'd gotten a hold of you," I say and walk over to Tramp, who looks nothing like the dog who was just about to have a teenager for a snack only moments ago. Maybe, it's because I'm holding an oatmeal cookie and he really loves that shite. Usually, we share—much to his dismay, of course.

Coffee to Go

Fun fact: It you jerk off; you'd better throw the paper towel in the bin. If not, it will be eaten and it's not nearly as sexy as when a gorgeous woman swallows your come. You just want to throw up.

I've *not* gotten used to Tramp's five o'clock schedule and I'm really feeling like a parent. Early mornings, not enough sleep—I'm a walking zombie. I'm never ever having children and since I can't get laid anyway that works out nicely. He's expensive like hell too. Vet, food, ridiculously large and expensive orthopaedic bed, toys, stimulation gadgets, and a new car. A two-person sportscar is not proper transportation for a dog that keeps growing and growing and growing…Unless I want to get fined or end up on YouTube. I don't want either. That's why I own a Range Rover. I'm only *slightly* bitter.

It should help me; it's July and the sun gets up at about five and it's brighter outside, but it doesn't. Also, July doesn't necessarily mean summer—it's still fucking cold this early. I see the angry women often but only at a distance. One morning, I even turned around and went the other way because I couldn't stand Tramp's excitement if he saw her.

For some reason, he really likes her. I only like to look at her—ass and tits that is. And from a safe distance.

I'm out of coffee today because I was reckless and left it on the kitchen table before I showered and got dressed. When I came back into the kitchen twenty minutes later, there was grounded coffee all over the floor and the container was across the room. The pet detective declared death by tail. I almost feel dead too when I drag my ass into the coffee shop on my way to work. I'm so tired I didn't even have the energy to be mad at Tramp who looked like he knew he could be in trouble. I have a feeling I left a very confused dog behind when I swiped up the coffee and just walked out the door without a word. But now, I feel *so* guilty. Dogs can do that to you.

I get in line just behind a gorgeous curvy woman with wavy chestnut hair, great tits, really great ass...wait a minute...She faces me and look at me with huge green eyes. She has long, full eyelashes, pert nose, and her pale pink lips in smiling slightly. Fuck, she's so sexy, my cock immediately stirs. Yup, it's the angry woman from the park.

"You look human and dressed today, I'm *almost* impressed," she says politely—and slightly mockingly.

"You're smiling today, I'm *definitely* impressed."

"Maybe I'm smiling because you're not wearing pj and little else?"

"Ouch, that hurts."

"Your ass *is* great—I'll give you that."

"Told you."

"That you did."

"It was a bit cold showing it off that morning, though."

"Why didn't you wear pants?"

"Because I was hoping to go back to sleep when I got home." Besides, I don't use underwear but that's none of her business.

"Has that ever happened?"

"No."

"So, you're just delusional?"

"Often."

"Why?"

"The alternative is too depressing."

"What's the alternative?"

"Accepting I won't be spending the day napping, eating random things, fucking a unicorn, and licking my own balls."

"Would that make you happy?"

"Licking my balls probably would. Tramp seems happy enough."

"Is that what he does all day?"

"I think so."

"Sounds cosy."

"Yeah, somebody definitely got the phrase about a dog's life wrong." She chuckles and I smile at her. I most certainly prefer this to the angry version of her in the park. It probably helps I haven't called her a tramp or mocked her tattoo today. I'd still like to lick it though. I'd like to lick something else too. I look at her and I wonder what it would be like to taste the sweet paradise I'm certain she has between her legs. Knees over my shoulders, make her beg, hear *my* name as I suck her clit and tease her with my tongue. God, I'd like that, and I'm not even embarrassed about it. Told you I need sex. Besides, a man can dream.

The line has moved us to the counter and I'm looking so much forward to the coffee *that* is almost embarrassing.

"Flat white to go," she asks the barista.

"Filter black to go, I'm buying," I say and hold out my credit card. She looks at me questioningly, the barista doesn't, and he quickly makes our coffee. We both say thank you as I take the cups and hand the flat white to the usually angry woman when we're outside.

"Thank you."

"I owe you an apology," I say.

"I'll get over it. But you owe your dog an apology for naming him Tramp."

"He chose it," I insist.

"He did?" She asks and I nod.

"First time I saw him, he didn't respond to his name, but when I told him he looked like The Tramp, he came running."

"Huh," she says. "What was his name?"

"Henry."

"Henry?"

"Yeah, my grandfather named him before he died. It was his dog."

"That explains it, you don't look like a dog person."

"Really?" I ask a bit insulted and forget I'd agreed with her about a year ago. Told you, dog owners are crazy.

"Really."

"I've had him for about a year, doesn't that qualify?"

"He's survived and he looks healthy, I'll give you points for that."

"I've survived too, do I get more points?" I ask and she shakes her head laughing.

"No, you don't. He's gorgeous."

"You're joking. He's ugly."

"Charming."

"Said no one ever."

"I just did," she smiles at me and damn, if that's not a pretty sight. Sigh.

"I'm Simon," I say and hold out my hand.

"Ginny. No liquor jokes and no Harry Potter jokes," she warns me.

"Don't worry, you're far more beautiful."

"Ugh…a player, I should've known."

"I'm not a player."

"Yeah right."

"Really. I've got a furry cockblocker at home."

"Shave before you go out."

"Funny," I deadpan. "I'm talking about Tramp."

"So, it's his fault?"

"It is. Last time I brought a woman home, he was howling even worse than when we ruin the upstairs neighbour's party." Ginny bursts out laughing. "It did kind of ruin the moment."

"He didn't like her?"

"I don't know, but at least he didn't eat her thong." Ginny almost chokes on her coffee, and I try very hard not to stare at her mouth as she licks her lips. I'm suddenly desperate for a taste of flat white.

"He's done that?" She asks.

"Chewed them to death at least."

"So, he likes a snack?" She says with a shrug and a suggestive smile, and I answer it with a dirty smile of my own.

"Don't we all?"

It's sort of nice being with a woman and not be desperate. Well, I am desperate, but since I'm not going to fuck Ginny, and particularly not in the middle of the street, I can relax and enjoy the conversation. Mostly. Who am I kidding? Not at all.

Ginny's wearing a loose poncho in sheer fabric, so I can't see much of her—only delicious curves. Still, my primal brain is stirring. It knows perfectly well I haven't had sex in ages, and it also remembers perfectly well how Ginny looks in her running gear. She looks absolutely fuckable and if her tattoo really says 'please fuck me harder'—I doubt it does—I'm all for it. Also, I'd still love to lick her everywhere. I should *not* be dreaming about that right now.

"We've seen you often at the park," I squeak.

"Say hi, and wear your running shoes next time," she suggests.

"You run every day?"

"Pretty much, sometimes, I just walk."

"Why so early? It's insane."

"I like the peace and I need the air. Once I'm off work, I can't drag myself anywhere."

"You should get a dog, then you don't have a choice. Three times a day."

"You don't have a garden?" I shake my head.

"Apartment."

"Ouch, that's got to be fun."

"Not really. But at least I don't have to go to the gym." I'm not even kidding.

I've always let Tramp set the length of our walks. I've read puppies can overexert themselves and I might've been a reluctant dog owner—I still am sometimes—but I had no intentions of walking him to death. I might regret that decision once in a while. I've only carried him home once—I'm not doing that ever again. Now, I walk at least ten miles a day, and now *I'm* the reason we don't walk any further. So, I'm in great walking and running form. As for the rest of the training…it's kind of difficult doing sit-ups and push-ups because every time I get near the floor, Tramp thinks it's because I want to play.

I've seen clips of a guy doing push-ups with a Golden Retriever on his back. Call me a wimp but Tramp's not a fucking Retriever—he's a hundred pound plus, restless monster dog, and I'm not bloody Superman. However, I must give him some credit about training. He has a knotted rope, and he really likes to tug it like his survival depends upon it. After a year of tugging that blasted rope, my biceps are as hard and almost as large as a bowling ball. Almost. I'm still working on making him do push-ups like I've seen a police dog do on YouTube. I have a feeling he thinks police dogs are stupid. But I'm not giving up on this and I have a special plan for tonight. It's called bribe and it works really well with dogs.

"Are you a good runner?" I ask and Ginny shrugs.

"Completed a few half marathons."

"Really?" She nods. "I don't believe you," I tease, and she rolls her eyes at me. She hands me her coffee and I take it without even considering it. She pulls her phone from her bag and scrolls through a lot of photos before showing me the screen.

"See? That was last year." Oh, I see all right. It's a photo of Ginny with a medal around her neck. She's wearing tights, a short top, and a huge grin. She's got a runner's slim physique if it wasn't for her big tits and perky ass. She's got slightly visible abs, but they're soft and feminine and utter delicious. I can't wait to lick and kiss my way along the smooth indents. Right, like that's ever going to happen.

"You won?"

"No," she snorts. "The medal is for finishing."

"Photoshop," I declare, and she playfully punches my arm before putting the phone back in her bag and retrieves her coffee. "All year round and weekends too?" I ask and she shakes her head.

"Too dark in winter and usually I go home on weekends."

"What does that mean?"

"I have a house in the country, about four hours from here by train. During the week, I sleep on my friend's couch."

"Why is that?"

"I work here, I can't afford two homes, and I don't want to get rid of my house." She turns left and I stop.

"I'm that way," I say and point straight ahead. Only I don't want to stop talking to her.

"Thanks for the coffee."

"You're welcome. Nice talking to you."

"You too." She smiles at me and then turns and continues down the street. And I just stand there like a lovesick puppy looking at her ass—I see the irony. I need to get laid. Bad.

*

When I get home after work, I'm greeted with a happy Tramp, he's wagging his entire body madly.

"Miss me?" I ask as I rub his sides furiously.

Delighted whimper.

"I missed you too."

Intense wagging.

"I need to change."

Delighted groan and semi-bark.

I go into the bedroom and do a quick inspection of the apartment on the way. Everything looks the same as when I left it this morning, and for a dog owner that's pretty much like winning the lotto. I quickly change from nice jeans to old jeans and favour a sweater to the shirt and blazer I was wearing at work. When I get back into the hallway Tramp has his entire head down my computer bag.

"Tramp," I snap, and he jerks back and pulls out the bag of treats I've brought home for this evening's push-up experiment. The strap of the computer bag is around his neck, but he doesn't seem to notice. The treats are so smelly I've wrapped it in two additional plastic bags, but apparently that wasn't enough to disguise the smell. Maybe he's part Bloodhound too? Tramp finding the treats leaves me with no idea how I'm going to hide this from him when he's home alone tomorrow. I imagine a lot of disastrous scenarios and I might need to bring the treats to work with me. And doesn't that just sound terrific? I hold out my hand.

"Let go."

Stubborn look.

"Let go."

Fuck you.

"Let go."

Looking anywhere but at me.

"Let *go*."

All right, dammit.

He walks slowly towards me and leaves the plastic bag in my hand.

"Good boy."

Fuck you.

I put the bag in the cupboard, and I see his eyes following every movement I make. I'm definitely bringing that to work tomorrow. I take the computer bag from his neck.

"Get the leash."

He dashes to the basket by the door and picks up the leash, then he sits his bum down by the front door and waits impatiently as I spend three seconds sticking my feet into my worn Timberland boots. When I spend another three seconds putting the hoodie on, he stands and starts tapdancing. After ten seconds, I'm ready to go to the park and I've been forever labelled as the slowest dog owner ever.

I know Ginny runs in the morning, but I can't help looking for her—even if I'm not wearing my running shoes. If she was here, I'd run to hell and back in Timberlands and I'm certain Tramp would follow. Maybe I could leave him there…in hell I mean.

I'm distracted because I look for Ginny and Tramp makes me take the long way round the lake. A five-mile walk was *not* what I had planned for tonight at all. After all, I have a plan, or an experiment at least.

When we finally get home, I don't feed Tramp, I'm counting on he'll be even more interested in the treats if he's about to keel over from hunger. I'm never ever telling other dog owners about this—they'll probably bring out their pitchforks because I'm such a monster.

I take a deep breath and then I open the magic bag. In the bag are fish treats and I want to throw up at the smell. Apparently, I'm a bit squeamish and I didn't even know this before I got a dog. The manufacturer of this hellish treat promises it's good for just about everything—digestion, mobility, brain, eyes, energy. Not sure energy is a good thing when it comes to Tramp. The treats are even gluten free and contains Omega 3—and I'm pretty sure Tramp doesn't give a shite about that. But the stench, of course, already has his attention, and he's sitting down in front of me.

"Push-ups," I say.

Cocks his head.

"Stand." He knows this one.

Standing up.

"Down." He knows this one too.

Lies down.

"Good boy," I praise and give him a treat. I've definitely got his full attention as I bring out another foul-smelling reward. God, they're horrible. I get down on the floor on my stomach and when I press up on my arms I say. "Stand."

Standing up. Eyes on snack.

"Down."

Lies down.

"Up."

Stands up, forgetting he doesn't know what "up" means.

"Down."

Lies down.

I manage seven push-ups like this before Tramp starts whimpering. He's also drooling on the floor—pretty impressive considering he's doing push-ups at the same time. I've got a really smart dog.

Do you know that Oliver Stone movie 'Natural Born Killers' from 1994? There's a quote there that's been my mantra from the first day I got Tramp home and tried to teach him new tricks: "Repetitions work (David). Repetitions work (David)." Repetitions *have* worked, so we do another two rounds of push-ups before I can't stand the stench of fish treats any more.

I sit at the floor that night and pet Tramp's large head, he's placed on my lap.

"You did good."

Raises an eyebrow.

"I met Ginny today."

No reaction.

I dare not tell him she's the woman from the *park*, because then he thinks we'll be going for a walk, and we definitely aren't.

"She thinks you're charming."

Raises head in confusion.

"I'm sorry if I've made you feel ugly."

Huge paw on my lap, barely missing my cock.

"She's really pretty when she's not sweating and angry." Honestly, only angry. A sweaty Ginny makes me think about sex, and I'd just *love* to make *her* sweat. Come to think of it, angry works too. Her eyes flash when she is pissed off, and any man would love to be the receiving end of the pain she would administer. Tie me down, smack my ass, and make me beg.

Cock of head.

"I'll introduce you properly the next time you meet."

Cock of head to the other side.

"You remember the angry woman?"

Tentative wagging.

"From the…" I just barely stop myself from saying park.

Smug look.

Told you, he's an asshole.

*

I meet with Hugh, Jeff, Matt, and Pete at the coffee shop next morning. It's Saturday and even if Tramp's already pulled my ass out of bed early this morning, we're all going to the park today. I'm running a bit late, and Tramp think it's a terrific idea jogging to the coffee shop. I've got some great friends. They might tease me relentlessly about Tramp and the changes he's made in my life, but they also go to the park with us, and they readily accept cards and beers has to be at my place because of Tramp. Of course, that also leaves cleaning up after poker night to someone else and that's very motivational for any man. They pet him and entertain him—mostly for their own pleasure—and they accept at least fifty percent of my conversation is about him. Dog owners are crazy—now they know too.

I'm wearing leather trainers, ripped jeans, a grey T-shirt and my obligatory five o-clock shadow even if it's only ten in the morning. Hugh teases me about it and says I should just grow a beard like a lumber jack or real man—he has one of course—but, honestly, you *don't* cover up bone structure like mine. I've got no underwear on and no socks either. I love it when the weather is warm enough for only T-shirt and showing off my tattoos. I've got a dragon on my right upper arm and its long tail ends at my lower arm. On my left upper arm, I have naturalistic looking skulls clouded in mist—this was my first one and I got it when I turned eighteen because I thought it looked cool—I still like it. On my lower left arm, I have a large rose and before Tramp started spending all of my money, I wanted to get more tattoos to connect the two. But right now, there're no more tattoos for me. And Ginny has a tramp stamp. I'd better stop dreaming about licking it or I'll have a hard-on by the time I get to the coffee shop.

"There he is," Hugh hollers delightedly as soon as I step inside the coffee shop. They sit at a table, and I appreciate they've waited for me. Outside, Tramp let out a happy bark and pulls the leash—and the lamp post.

"Sit," I say and points towards the ground, even if I'm inside the coffee shop, and he smacks his bum to the ground. I can still see him because he's not exactly shorter when sitting down.

"Where's the photographer?" Pete asks.

"Is it because Tramp actually did, what I told him you want a picture?"

"You look like a jeans-commercial," he smirks, and I shove him so hard he tumbles of his chair.

"Funny. Get the bloody coffee," I grumble and sit down on his chair. Pete laughs and I just hate that look on his face, because he looks like he might have yet another idea for my jeans commercial nickname. One year, they gave me a denim shirt and a white T-shirt and a cowboy hat from a toy store for my birthday.

"What's with you? You look even more tortured than usual," Jeff says.

"The angry woman from the park is a fox," I moan. I've told them about my run-ins with Ginny—they think it is hilarious of course.

"What are you talking about?" Matt asks.

"The angry one with the great tits and ass. She's a fox."

"Duh, if she's a fox that's a given…" Matt says.

"No, it's not," Hugh scoffs and I turn to him—at least he knows what I'm talking about. A woman can be foxy for numerous reasons, but Matt's really not that creative when it comes to women.

"How does she look?" Jeff asks.

"Lickable," I mutter and Matt guffaws.

"You need sex, my friend," he says and claps me on the shoulder.

"Tell me something I don't know."

"How does she look?" Jeff repeats.

"Chestnut hair, green eyes…"

"Great colours for a fox," Matt interjects.

"Cute nose, pale, pouty lips."

"Who looks like that?" Pete asks from behind me. He's brought the coffee and I even see a paper bag that indicates he's bought Tramp an oatmeal cookie. Tramp likes it better when Pete buys the cookies for him, because he gets to eat all of it. And that's how I lose yet another popularity contest.

We go to the park, and Hugh holds Tramp's leash. It feels funny I'm not the one, but I really appreciate my friends helping me with Tramp once in a while. Unfortunately, none of them is up for babysitting—not even so I can get laid.

We find an open space in the sun and sit down. Matt and Hugh play with Tramp while the rest of us sip our coffee and watch as Tramp runs, jumps, catches, and fetches the frisbee with endless energy and talent. It would've been easier throwing a ball, but balls don't have a great survival-rate around Tramp. Jeff can attest to that since Tramp tackled him once by running straight into his groin. The basketball didn't survive that day either and poor Jeff was very disillusioned when we left the park. Also, he was limping and holding his balls.

We lie on the grass and enjoy the sight of summer—meaning the sight of scantly clothed women—and apart from being drenched, because Tramp's still practicing drinking from a bottle, life feels pretty good right now. There's a gadget you can buy so dogs can drink more easily from a bottle, but you heard the keyword in that sentence, right? 'Buy.' I fucking hate the pet industry.

"So, what are you doing to do about your foxy lady?" Matt asks with a huge grin while he's wagging his eyebrows.

"Besides enjoy it when she's not breathing fire? Not a God damn thing."

A Dog's Life

Fun fact: Dogs will lick everything.

I might have lied to Matt, when I told him I wasn't going to do anything about Ginny, because I start wearing my track pants and running shoes when we go to the park in the morning despite the evil glare I get from Tramp because it takes me a few minutes to get dressed. I feel slightly more human when I'm not in my pj, but not much. We meet her often and run with her. We talk, but not much, because she's a great runner and keeps a steady pace even for me. And Tramp *loves* Ginny. I mean *really loves* her. Maybe there's gun dog in Tramp too, because whenever he sees her, he stalks after her like a maniac. His mixed breeding could easily include some sort of hound, so maybe he thinks she is a fox too. It often takes me a while to catch up with them. I love looking at her ass and it's very motivating running behind her. It's probably mostly because my sex-life is non-existent. It pretty much has been since I brought Tramp home about a year ago.

What used to be my sex-life is now my dog's life. That's probably why a dog's life is considered a bad thing. It's got nothing to do with the dog, but just the general lack of sex for the owner. I try not to leave Tramp alone too much, I don't think it's fair, so I don't go out as much as I used to. As a result, my sex-life has been quickies and I'm not taking it anymore. Tonight's the night!

"I'll be back soon," I say and pat his head. It's Friday night, it's nine o'clock and I've taken him for a long walk. We've played, he's gotten food, and I've brought home a huge bone for him to keep him entertained. But *I* need to be entertained too and so does my cock! It takes me less than two hours, including three drinks, one dance, small-talk, and a hell of a lot of compliments and eye-fucking until Mandy says she'd love to see my apartment, despite I tell her I have a very large dog.

I almost stumble up the stairs because I'm kissing Mandy at the same time—I try to, at least. She's the octopus-kind of woman—you know, the kind who sucks your face off and her hands are everywhere. I don't care, tonight I like cephalopods.

Tramp whines happily when we stumble through the door. I try to pet him, I wave him off, and try kiss Mandy at the same time. I think it works.

"Simon, you're so big," Mandy moans as her tentacles grab my cock. Yeah, yeah, thank you, I know, I don't care. I haven't gotten properly laid for over a year and I don't give a shite, what she's saying right now. I just want to fuck.

"Let's get you on the bed and I'll show you how big," I groan before I kiss her again. She giggles happily—but not annoyingly—jumps up and wraps her legs around my waist. That's exactly where I want them and I grind against her despite walking, despite wearing clothes, despite I think we might have an accident any time. Right now, I don't give a shite.

I lay her down on the bed and I keep kissing her mouth. God, I need this. I grind my hard-on against her core, and she moans delighted. I can't wait to strip her, and I can't wait to fuck her. This is going to be *so good*. She grabs my ass and pull me even closer, and I'd better slow this down a bit. I need to come, when I'm inside her and not my jeans. Lack of sex will unfortunately turn a grown and *extremely* capable man into a teenager if he's not careful.

"You've got a great ass," she says delighted and pinches me.

"So, I've been told," I say, because I really *do* know—Ginny told me too—and pull of Mandy's blouse. I throw it on the floor and hope my thoughts of Ginny will leave the bed as well.

We kiss clumsily while we're tearing at each other's clothes. My sweater is the first to go. I'm so turned on I can hardly think. It might be desperation and not horniness, but the outcome is the same—not pretty. I ignore the sound of fabric ripping when I pull her skirt down—she does too—and she moans delighted when I grab her bare ass. She accidently pokes my eye when she rips my T-shirt of, but I don't care—I don't need two eyes to fuck.

I stagger of the bed and shrug off my jeans. Mandy's eyes widen accordingly when she sees my hard cock and it jerks in anticipation.

"Oh, Simon," she pants and then she tears at her underwear. I've got to say, I've never ever seen a woman get naked so fast and I truly appreciate it. She's spread out on my bed and my mouth is almost watering even if I'm going to fuck her with my cock and not my tongue. I'll gladly do that later, but right now anticipation is killing me. I *need* to fuck her, I'm not sure I'll survive it if I don't.

"Show me your pretty pussy," I ask as I jerk off loosely. If I yank my cock any harder it'll probably blow, but Mandy's got another idea as she leans forward and grabs my cock like a toddler reaching for ice cream.

"I want you inside me," she moans throatily. Not a problem. Not. At. All.

I clench my teeth as I roll the condom on, my cock is practically twitching to get started and my hands are shaking. I've only just put on the condom, and then I'm on the bed with her. I suppose I should kiss her or at least look at her face, but I just *can't* right now. I groan loudly as I push into her. God, I've missed pussy. And I've missed fucking in a bed and not a somewhere in semi-public because I just need to get off.

"Oh God, Simon," she pants.

"You feel amazing," I sigh in sheer relief and ecstasy as I start to move inside her. Thank fucking God for muscle memory.

A loud whine sounds from the other side of the door, but I ignore it, as I pull out and flex my hips, pushing my cock deep into Mandy again. Shite, this is good. I love pussy, I love fucking—I really do. Something bumps loudly against the door. I ignore it. I don't care if the whole damn building is falling down around us, I'm that desperate to fuck.

"Like that, Simon." Mandy is starting to pant desperately. Her nails are digging into my ass as I fuck her and that feels pretty spectacular too. My focus wavers when there's a loud thud on the door and something cracks. Oh no. No no no no no no no no no no, this is bad, this is very very bad, this is really bad…An insane howl, that would do very well as a

Judgement Day siren fills the hallway. It sounds like that singing Husky I saw on YouTube. At the time I thought that was fucking hilarious. Now? Not so much. Mandy moans delighted—apparently, only one of us is distracted by the noise Tramp is making.

"Shut up, Tramp," I growl as I attempt to ignore the howling and keep fucking. It's not that easy—especially not when Mandy stiffens beneath me.

"What did you call me?"

"Not you, baby. The dog." I add the endearment because the last thing I want right now is for her to get pissed at me and leave. Not yet anyway. I need to come first. Then she can leave.

Twenty seconds later, I give up. I pull my stone-fucking-hard cock out of Mandy's soft, wet pussy. I need to put my dog to bed—you see what I mean about it's like having a baby? Besides, if I don't make him shut up, I might get evicted. My landlord and neighbours have been very patient with me and Tramp so far because I do what I can to keep him quiet. They accept an occasionally bark and howl, but I don't think they'll appreciate it if I just let him serenade everybody because I'm having sex.

"Bed," I say sternly. He looks at me and then I see his snout move slightly as he sniffs the air. I'm standing naked in front of him, I'm only wearing the condom I just had in Mandy's soaked pussy—no fucking wonder he's interested. "Bed," I growl as he licks his snout. If his tongue gets anywhere near my cock I'm putting him down, I shite you not. He sulks all the way to the large and ridiculously expensive orthopaedic bed. A daily reminder that dog owners are idiots.

"Sorry about that," I say to Mandy as I close the bedroom door and lock it. She's lying on the bed, she's scrolling through her phone with a vacant expression, looking bored. She turns to me and smiles.

"Come here and make it up to me, stud." The way she's holding out her arms clearly indicated she wants some kind of attention before I fuck her again and I suppose that's fair enough, but, honestly, I just want a release that's not by my own hand. I wasn't always this selfish, but it's been so long since I've had a woman in my bed, I feel like I might die, if I don't get to fuck her within the next few seconds.

I kiss her deeply and I keep kissing her, hoping I can sneak my cock into her pussy again without having to wait, or work any harder for it. And thank God, it works, because she spreads her legs for me, and I push into her as deep as she can take me. I'm still hard even if I've put Tramp to bed and that just shows the enormity of my desperation to have sex.

"Oh God, like that," she squeals and I want to slam my hand over her mouth to make her shut the hell up so she doesn't draw Tramp's attention. I kiss her instead, hoping to keep the noise down. Normally, I like a noisy woman in bed, but right now I wish she was a secret undercover agent on a mission. A Husky-worthy concert starts up in the hallway and I lift my head and clench my teeth. I want to keep fucking, I *need* it.

"Simon," she pants—and it's not in a good way.

"Just ignore him." Right now, I don't give a shite if I get evicted. I'll live in the streets, and I'll eat Tramp when I get hungry because it'll be his fault, we're homeless.

"I can't do this," she shrieks. She pushes my shoulder and I regretfully roll of her.

The door slams behind her only three minutes later and I think I might cry. I stalk into the hallway and look at Tramp.

"You're a menace," I growl. He rolls onto his back and is grinding against his ridiculously large expensive orthopaedic bed. His lipstick dick is poking out, my hard-on is no more. Well done, Tramp.

The Angry Woman

Fun fact: Women aren't better multitaskers than men— they're just doing more work.

Tramp keeps growing and I'm starting to wonder if he's not supposed to stop at some time. I've looked at a lot of grow charts and it's safe to say he's in the category of giant dogs. He's almost hundred fifty pounds, thirty-two inches, and he almost looks like a really buff Irish Wolfhound on steroids. But then there're the ears which almost look like a Great Dane's if they are not cropped. His tail looks like it belongs to a scruffy German Shephard, and he whines like a Husky. He's got the neck like a giraffe, a tongue like an anteater, and he's an asshole in the cat kind of way. I'm not any closer determining his breed than the vet was. I'm still not paying for having him DNA tested. With my luck, it'll come up 'inconclusive,' and *that* I believe.

At just over two years old, he pretty much follows the growth chart for Irish Wolfhound—meaning he's a big fucker. And slightly heavier. I've considered Mastiff too, but he seems to have a lot more energy, and he's slimmer and a bit taller than the Mastiffs we've met.

Do you know the movie 'Pirates of the Caribbean: Dead Man's Chest' from 2006? It's the second 'Pirates of the

Caribbean' movie and it was directed by Gore Verbinski and produced by Jerry Bruckheimer. It's kind of funny. There was a dog in that movie—it was in the first movie as well. A mongrel that carried the keys for the jail, and it was last seen running to escape a native tribe on an island. It kind of looked like Tramp does, only Tramp is larger and uglier—didn't really think uglier was possible.

*

I've not given up trying to get laid and I meet Matt, Hugh, Jeff, and Pete at a bar. They promise they've invited women too. It's never been much trouble for me to pick up women, but at my present state of abstinence I'll consider anything that makes it faster and easier a bonus.

As soon as I've made it to the table and greeted my friends, Jeff gets up with a dramatic flourish. My bet is he's been here for a while and my bet is he's already at least five shots into the evening.

"I'll get beers. And drinks for the ladies," Jeff proclaims generously. He should be feeling generous, he just got a raise—and he doesn't own a dog either.

"Sure, you got that?" Hugh mocks.

"Of course," Jeff scoffs. "I can multitask."

"The hell you can!" Matt says with an exaggerated roll of his eyes.

"Hell, yeah, I can look at two tits at the same time."

"Behind you," Hugh whispers, and Jeff spins on his heels only to face two women.

"There you are," he says with a grin and acts like he didn't just make a stupid joke. He hugs both of them, they obviously know each other and that probably explains why they don't look like they want to smack him.

"Charming as always," the brunette says and accepts the kiss Jeff plants on her cheek. Jeff ignores her comment and turn towards us.

"Ladies, this is Simon, Matt and Pete." He points to us as he makes the introduction. "Gentlemen, this is Lindsey and Deborah." Ladies and gentlemen? Jeff is looking to get laid tonight too, that's for sure! Hugh gets up and hugs both of them and it suddenly makes more sense the women agreed to come here. No woman in her right mind accepts an invitation to go to a bar with his friends from Jeff—Hugh is *slightly* more sensible.

Lindsey is a cute Asian woman. Her leather pants are skin-tight, the heels of her red shoes can be used as a murder weapon, her blouse is open to her navel and showing off her pink bra. The way she's looking at me my guess is, she's definitely looking for the same kind of fun I am. Deborah is curvy, has brown, curly hair, and wears glasses that makes her look like a naughty librarian. She's got a wide mouth and full lips and it's almost *too* easy imagining a blow job hidden behind a bookcase. Tight, short skirt, thigh high boots that emphasise her long legs and wouldn't I just love to have them wrapped around my hips? She doesn't even have to take off the boots—I'd actually prefer it if she didn't. She licks her full bottom lip and look me over, it's subtle, and not quite as obvious as Lindsey did, but I get the message.

"Who's going to dance with me?" Lindsey asks and I'm up from my chair and manage to punch Matt in the stomach in two seconds flat. He gives me the evil eye, but that doesn't change the fact that it's *me* Lindsey pulls towards the dance floor.

Lindsey squeals delighted as I spin her on the dancefloor. God, I've missed dancing. I've missed having my hands on a beautiful woman, feel her touch me as she gets bolder. I hear her slight gasp when she feels my semi and I groan accordingly when she squeezes my cock. This is going to be a great night—I can feel it.

Before the dance is over, she's almost climbing me like a tree, and I practically stumble when we get to the table. Jeff has bought beer and cocktails that look like someone has forced a rainbow into a glass. I straighten myself in the last moment before I fall over and come almost face to face with a woman. Wavy chestnut hair hangs down both sides of a cleavage that might be the Bermuda Triangle. Jesus.

Do you know that baseball movie 'Bull Durham' from 1988? It's starring Kevin Costner, Susan Sarandon and Tim Robbins. It was directed—but more importantly written—by Ron Shelton. I don't give a shite about baseball, I really don't, but this movie is one of the best I've ever seen because of the dialogue. And yes, of course I know the 'Believe' speech by heart. The dialogue that comes to mind right now is not the Believe speech, but a comment made by rookie Ebby Calvin 'Nuke' LaLoosh about how the V-shape of a woman's pussy is The Bermuda Triangle because a man could get lost in there and never be heard from again. After seeing this cleavage, I *know* that's not the only place a man could get lost.

I recite the Believe speech *and* the dialogue about the Bermuda Triangle in my head before I finally manage to look at her face.

"Ginny?" I say surprised when I've managed to raise my eyes from her tits to her face. Now I'm gaping at her face, and I have no idea how the hell I'm going to pick up my jaw that has just hit the floor. She's wearing make-up, her eyes look even larger and greener than usual, and lipstick that makes her lips look something I should definitely suck on. And lick. And have wrapped around my cock. I've never wanted to fuck a woman so much in my entire life.

"Do you two know each other?" Hugh asks with a curious look.

"Yeah, we've met at the park," Ginny says and Jeff's face lights up. I know what he's going to say, but I don't have time to stop him.

"You're the angry fox," Pete exclaims and beats Jeff to it. I'm surrounded by idiots.

"Excuse me?" She snaps and my inside cringes. Ginny thought I was an asshole when she believed I called her a tramp, but really…she's got no idea how big of an asshole I am.

"Simon said he met an angry, foxy lady in the park with great tits."

"And ass," Hugh helpfully adds. I just groan.

"Ginny said she met an insane guy in a pj with a huge cock," Deborah says like she's just won the lottery. Well, at least, Ginny had acknowledged *some* part of me besides my ass. She doesn't seem to find me as charming as most women do, so I'm actually starting to wonder if she is a lesbian. I know, I know…I'm conceded, but, honestly, have you seen me?

"You did?" I ask.

"You have," she says and shrugs. Everyone at the table bursts out laughing—except for Lindsey who slides her hand over my jeans and grabs my cock so hard it makes me humph. Damn, she's handsy.

"I can't wait," she purrs, and Pete clears his throat.

"Linds, do you think you can wait a bit longer?" He asks as I peel her fingers one by one from my cock. It's not an easy task. I'm all for sexually aggressive women, but if she dismembers me, she's not going to get fucked later.

I know I'm going to fuck Lindsey when the night is over, but it's Ginny I can't stop staring at as the night progresses. The guys flirt with her, but casually and mostly to piss me off. And it's working. They send me a lot of grins from across the table—especially when Ginny slow-dances with Hugh. Only I shouldn't be pissed off, should I?

We drink a lot of beers and Lindsey downs cocktails like she's addicted to rainbows. Deborah drinks Chardonnay like it's lemonade and she looks like it's lemonade too—she doesn't seem affected at all. Ginny drinks *gin* and tonic—she left her liquified rainbow to Lindsey—and she is even more attractive when tipsy. She giggles and her cheeks and the tip of her nose is slightly red. I've licked and sucked a lot of women's body-parts, but I must say it's the first time I've ever considered sucking on a nose.

We stay at the bar until it closes at three in the morning. I've had so much fun, but my mind is counting the number of hours Tramp has been alone. Right now, he should be sleeping like he does every night—so why do I worry? I may even feel slightly…guilty…that I'm not there. While he's sleeping. Dog owners are crazy!

The fresh air outside feels like I'm hitting a brick wall. I instantly feel slightly more drunk but also refreshed at the same time. The air of the August night feels amazing, and I take deep breaths to soak it all in. I turn as Ginny comes out the door of the bar. She too looks like she soaks up the fresh air as well.

"Where are the others?"

"Wardrobe commotion," she says dismissively with a wave over her shoulder like she feels she's just made a narrow escape. We stand and wait in silence, and I've never been particularly good at that.

"Thanks for complimenting my cock," I finally say—and regret it instantly.

"Thanks for complimenting my ass and tits."

"We're just going to pretend tonight's conversation didn't happen the next time we meet, right?" I ask, and she nods.

"Right."

"Right," I repeat, because it was sort of awkward, and I'm still not certain if Ginny is a lesbian. But the thing about pretending? I already know I can't—I mean how the hell can I pretend I didn't see a cleavage like that?

"Yeah, bye." She waves stiffly and turns around and my gaze follows her to the taxi she's just flagged down. God, she's got a great ass, and the task of pretending just got a whole lot more difficult.

Lindsey comes staggering out the bar. Hiccups mix with laughter and I'm beginning to realise I won't be taking her home after all—she's too drunk.

"So sexy, Simon," she purrs. She leans into me and grabs my cock while she's kissing me. She clumsily attempts to open my jeans and thank God she's so drunk, or she might actually have succeeded. I usually don't flash my cock in public and so far, Ginny's the only woman I've flashed my ass.

"We need to get you home," I say as I manage to pull myself away from her.

"Noooo," she complains. "I want you to fuck me."

"You are too drunk, Lindsey."

"Am not." I look at her and she suddenly seems far more sober than she did only a moment ago. "I was just having a bit of fun," she pouts. She grabs the lapels of my jacket and looks up at me. She's drunk, yes—I am too—but she doesn't look like she doesn't know what she's doing.

"Are you sure?" She runs her fingers along my cock—she definitely knows what she's doing.

"Please, Simon." She kisses me again, she keeps kissing me, and I hear Matt whistling somewhere behind me. I don't even glance his way—I'm busy—and I don't respond to the farewell clap on my back either. My cock is about to burst through my jeans and that's when all sense and reason leaves the world.

"Promise me you know what you're doing."

"I know," she says with a smile. She pulls away from me and then promptly throws up on the pavement. Violently.

I've still not gotten laid and this time it isn't even Tramp's fault.

When I get home, Tramp is delighted to see me, and I praise him for being a good boy. We go for a short walk, and I've got to admit I sort of like it. I walk the city streets with my dog while the world around us is noisy, partying, throwing up, and fighting. Even the most drunk bastard seems to understand not to mess with Tramp when he's snarling to protect me. He might not want to admit it, but he likes me—I know he does! I feel good when I come home from our walk. I had a good time at the bar although it didn't turn out the way I expected. I can't stop thinking about Ginny and that's only a good thing when I'm in the shower.

On Saturday, we've only just come home from Tramp's afternoon walk when my phone rings with an unknown number.

"Hello?"

"Hey, Simon, it's Lindsey."

"Hey, how are you feeling?"

"Sorry about yesterday."

"It's all right. It happens."

"Want me to make it up to you?"

"Do you feel like making it up to me?"

"I definitely do." Then who I am to refuse her? I give her my address, and she says she'll be there in half an hour. I have time for a shower and a shave and for Googling if there's any way, I can get a sedative in ten minutes that'll knock out a horse sized animal for a few hours. In the end, I decide it's time for a chew bone so large it might've come from a dinosaur.

Despite his dinosaur-sized bone, Tramp gets up when the doorbell rings. Head and tail held high he's almost a good-looking fucker. Almost. I open the door for Lindsey. She's wearing a coat and lacquered leather stiletto boots that disappear under her coat. She almost looks like a stripper and I'm *not* going to complain about that at all. She holds out her hand and Tramp sniffs her. He's very selective about the people he likes, and it seems Lindsey falls into the official category 'I don't give a fuck about you'—another proof of his cat-like personality, because dogs are supposed to like everyone, right? Hopefully, his indifference lasts the rest of the night—I know the chew bone won't.

"You like dogs?" I ask her.

"No, but I'm used to them. My parents have American Bulldogs." Tramp rolls his eyes and goes to his large and ridiculously expensive orthopaedic bed where the unicorn is ready and waiting for him. I'm ready too, no doubt about that.

Lindsey rips open her coat and wow, that's…interesting. She's wearing a tiny leather bra. A few strings make it out for panties and there's an abundance of leather strings and buckles in between.

"I've been a bad girl, Simon," she says in a sultry voice.

"Have you now?"

"So bad." She drops the coat where she stands and gets down on all fours. She then proceeds crawling across the floor like a cat. I keep an eye on Tramp who's looking at her like she's some sort of alien—I've seen that look before. Safe to say Lindsey is in 'the fuck' category in more ways than one. I feel like telling him I have no idea what the hell she's doing either. Now that she's removed her coat, I see she's even wearing a collar, and I swear Tramp is eyeing it with bafflement, like he hasn't considered humans could wear one too.

I follow her into the bedroom, she's still on her knees when she rips my jeans open. I'm not quite hard yet—my cock is apparently as stunned as the rest of me is. She really has that cat impersonation going on as she starts licking my cock pretty much like a cat cleaning itself. Thank God, I'm desperate to fuck, if not my cock may have shrunk all the way into my abdomen. And thank God, she starts sucking me—

my cock definitely understands that. She almost sounds like she's purring when I start to harden in her mouth—until she almost chokes. She wipes her mouth with the back of her hand and somehow, she makes that look feline too. My cock is suddenly starting to have second doubts about this.

Lindsey crawls—yes, crawls—onto the bed like she's a cat looking for a place to get comfortable. She gets up on all fours and sways her back, so her ass is on full display.

"No kissing today, but you can bite me if you want," she says, looking over her shoulder at me.

"Really?" I'm not certain if this is supposed to be a good thing or not.

"*Anywhere* you like." Right. As I get on the bed behind her, she opens a buckle and removes one of the straps and that's all it takes for her to show me her asshole, pretty much like cats often do—hello to you too. "I need to be punished," she moans. I smack her ass, and she mews delighted—and loudly! I glance towards the door but so far there's no sign of Tramp and I hope it stays that way. Please let it stay that way.

Despite my desperation, I have no idea how long I can stay hard. God, my life is a tragedy! I don't know if I find her behaviour sexy or comical and that's a really bad thing considering the situation. I smack her ass absently and roam my bedside table for a condom. Lindsey doesn't seem to notice I'm distracted, because she mews and purrs and makes sounds, I didn't know any human could emit. She's clearly enjoying herself and she's clawing the sheets happily while I fumble with the condom.

"On your back, Simon," she demands and I obey instantly.

Cat or not, it feels fucking fantastic as she slides down and takes my cock into her. For some reason unknown to me her *pussy*—that word is hilarious right now—is wet and she's more than ready for *all* of me. For a moment I'm *so* thrilled…and then she emits a meow. An honest to God *meow*. A very loud one too. I'm not even surprised when I hear paws coming from the hallway—if I were Tramp, I'd want to investigate too. I close my eyes, place my hands on her hips, and think of England. Well, not quite, but I desperately want to think about something else—anything that'll keep my cock hard, honestly.

She rides me furiously and grinds down hard on me—and meows loudly. Her movements become more aggressive and thank fuck, she's got short nails, if not she would be shredding me as she sinks her fingers into my pecs. I'm definitely going to have bruises from this. I hear a whine from beside the bed and I open my eyes. Tramp is standing beside the bed, he's tapdancing like he doesn't know what to do. I understand him completely—I don't know what to do either. He lets out a moaning snarl that could be playful, but clearly reflects his confusion about the creature in my bed making weird noises. Honestly, I'm a bit confused too, but Lindsey is not deterred. She keeps fucking, she keeps meowing. Tramp's is humping the laundry basket by now and I have no idea what the hell *I'm* supposed to do. So, I just lie here.

She rides me until she orgasms and meows even louder. I'm totally stunned, and I have absolutely no idea how I've managed to stay hard this long. Fucking some sort of cat has never been om my bucket list.

"Simon, that was amazing," she purrs.

"Yeah," I say and hope I sound sufficiently pleased. I'm not. Not really. I didn't even come. I just want to take an old-fashioned woman to bed. One who doesn't mew, needs to be spanked, wants to be gagged, plays cat, or giggles like a maniac on coke. Maybe I'm getting old, but what the hell is wrong with missionary and kissing? My cock is soft, and I haven't even come. This is kind of an off day for me. This doesn't normally happen.

Tramp has rolled onto his side, the laundry basket is between his legs, he looks like he's cuddling it like any other guy does with…whatever…when he says thank you for the hot fuck.

When dogs hump, it's not necessarily sexually motivated, but I'll bet my ass it is now, and he's definitely over-stimulated. I am too—even without the release. I've been to the vet with Tramp—hear the ka-ching?—just to make sure there's no medical problems to explain the humping. There isn't. Of course not. I'm still debating whether I should neuter him or not. It might be practical but cutting of another 'guy's' balls—that's just…wrong. My own balls almost ache at the thought.

Remember when I told him if he was going to be my dog, he should learn it's better to fuck than look like a tramp? Yeah, well, he does too apparently. Shouldn't have told him that. The laundry basket was about the fifty-seventh in a long line of conquests. And I don't think he has finished. He's humped lamp posts, the couch, the unicorn of course, legs, rubbish bins, suitcases, cardboard boxes, bushes…the list goes on forever. He's a regular Casanova that one, and sadly he does better than me. While he was getting off with the unicorn and the laundry basket, I watched a woman dressed like a Roman sandal crawl around in my living room. She licked me like a cat cleaning itself and fucked me like she was a lion attacking a zebra—at least she didn't have claws. You should know that this is the strangest thing I've ever done!

I need to regain some sort of control over my life.

Furry Cockblocker

Fun fact: Dogs are often 'growers not showers.'

For some reason that has absolutely nothing to do with controlling my life, I keep wearing track pants and running shoes when we go to the park in the morning. I look for Ginny constantly and when I see her Wednesday morning I'm almost as thrilled as Tramp, and I feel in control of...absolutely nothing.

She turns her head and smiles brightly when Tramp runs past her, and I wave and increase my speed to catch up with her. We've talked a bit when we've been running together—me mostly—and among other things I've told her about the vet. This made her laugh so hard she had to stop running. She was also cute enough to blush on my behalf. I'd rather make her blush another way though. I've enlightened her on a lot of Tramp's escapades and for some reason she likes him even more because of them. I've even told her about the 'shite day' and meeting Laura in full uniform in the park. It feels comfortable running besides her again and the awkwardness from the bar is gone. So, naturally I can't help myself.

"You've got a great ass," I say when I've caught up with her. I'm probably putting my life on the line—but Ginny just laughs. She has a musical laughter that gives me goosebumps and I feel like laughing too whenever I hear it.

"Too. You mean I've got a great as *too* since I've already complimented yours."

"Want to see it again?"

"No."

"Please?" I beg, but she just laughs at me.

"I take it your endeavours to get laid this weekend didn't turn out the way you expected?"

"Of course not."

"Impressive."

"Why is that?"

"Lindsey was very determined to…" I don't let her finish.

"She threw up Friday. Luckily, before I got her home."

"So, you *did* get lucky?" Ginny laughs.

"Not the way I was hoping."

"What happened Saturday?"

"She kind of used me for a fuck-toy while singing some sort of twisted cat-duet with Tramp." Ginny starts laughing and she has to stop running not to stumble. God, she's cute.

"The duet is a new addition."

"She also threatened to come back another time with her toys and *tools*," I say and shudder violently.

"I never would have taken you for a prude."

"I'm not, but there's something in between Lindsey and prudish. A lot actually." Ginny laughs again and I can't help smiling, because I can see this can be somewhat funny. Now that it's hopefully over anyway.

"And you're in between?" She asks, and I nod.

"I think I'm getting old," I sigh.

"How old are you?"

"Twenty-seven."

"Pup. Just wait until you hit thirty."

"Don't think I'll survive that long," I sigh, and Ginny rolls her eyes at me.

"Race you, old man," she says and smacks my ass hard before she takes off in a sprint. I'm momentarily stunned, because my brain short-circuits, and I just want her to keep spanking me. *I'll* even wear a tiny leather bra and panties if she wants me to. Damn, I'm getting desperate. And maybe not so old and prudish as I thought only a moment ago.

I run after her. She's in great shape and it takes me longer than expected to catch up with her—as always. Before I reach her, Tramp breezes happily by both of us without even looking like he's trying at all. Asshole.

"You cheated," I complain loudly. I pick her up in a fireman's hold and spin around and Tramp barks happily and runs around me looking for a way to join the fun. I slap her ass and damn, I want to keep my hand there. And maybe I do for a few seconds. I want to spank her ass and grab it, as I fuck her—so much for missionary. I'm getting hard and that's a really bad idea when you're only wearing running shorts. I need to start wearing boxer briefs, duct tape, or something equally constricting.

"Tramp, help me," Ginny squeals and his happy barks turns slightly sinister. He jumps and I just have time to let go of Ginny before he punches me in the gut with his huge paws. I think I should cancel my roadside assistance subscription because if the Range Rover ever breaks down Tramp can push it all the way to a garage.

We stumble to the ground in a tangled mess of arms and legs and fur. Ginny is still laughing, so I take this as a sign that she's not hurt. You never know when Tramp is involved. I roll onto my back on the lawn and look at Ginny. She's on her stomach—got to appreciate the profile of her ass—and laughing at Tramp. He's got his front legs on the ground, his huge ass and wagging tail in the air and he's barking happily. I get up and hold my hand out and she takes it to get up. I have a flashback to the first day I met her, and I must admit right now I'd still very much like to fuck her in public in the middle of the gravel path busting my knees, with Tramp as an audience. It's a beautiful dream.

"Are you up for breakfast and coffee? My place?" I ask.

"Sure."

"It's been a long time since I've had a woman for breakfast."

"You're not having one today either. No biting." I know she's teasing me, but why did she have to say that? I feel flustered and slightly shy because in a moment my cock will be tenting my stupid running shorts. Just because she said 'biting.' I can imagine it so easily. Gently biting the insides of her thighs, or her nipples, or her neck when I sink my cock deep into her from behind...Goosebumps spread all over my body at the mere thought.

"That's not what I meant. There was an *over* missing from that sentence," I say defensively. I need to think of something else. Right now!

"Don't count on having me *over* breakfast."

"That's also not what I meant,"

"Not when breakfast is *over* either."

"That's still not what I meant," I groan.

"Do you need a shovel for the hole you're digging for yourself?" She asks, laughing. Tramp vigilantly raises his head and then he promptly starts digging where he stands. In a moment it'll be big enough for a dog owner mass grave.

"Oh no."

"What the hell is that about?" Ginny asks, looking confused.

"Tramp, enough!" I growl.

Questioning whine.

"Not every conversation is about you, God damn it."

Genuine confusion.

"My father taught him to…do the thing with his paws and the ground," I tell Ginny as I scrape my foot in an in vain attempt to cover some of the damage Tramp's done to the pristine park lawn. It's not really working out for me.

"Wow," Ginny says and then she turns her attention to Tramp. "You're a smart boy, aren't you?"

Bark.

"Sit."

Slams bum to the ground.

"Down."

Lies down.

"Sit."

Gets up fast and sits proudly with his chest puffed out.

"Good boy," she praises, and Tramp gets up and accepts her—exaggerated—praise. His entire body is wagging, and he looks so delighted with her praise I'm almost jealous. Almost. Ginny reaches back towards me, she's not looking—her attention is fixed on Tramp—which means she's groping me.

"That feels so good," I moan. My hips move on their own accord and in a moment, I'm going to have difficulties concealing my hard-on.

"Treat," she says and snaps her fingers without looking back.

"Let's go home first," I moan. "I'll give you any treat you want." She finally looks at me and then rolls her eyes when she notices my 'growing enthusiasm.'

"For Christ's sake, Simon."

"Hey, *you* groped *me*," I say defensively.

"Don't you have treats in your pocket?"

"Yeah."

"I was looking for the treats."

"You found it, only not for the dog." She groans and shakes her head and then she turns her attention towards Tramp.

"It's your horny owners fault, you don't get a treat," she tells Tramp, but he seems to be content with her praise. Image that.

"He's not exactly starving, you know?"

"Still, he should be rewarded."

"What about me?"

"What about you? What have *you* done?"

"Fed him, trained him, made him a fitness freak." Fitness freak is not quite accurate, but I want her to ask about it—so I can brag.

"Fitness freak?" She frowns and looks at me like she thinks I'm making it up. "How's that?" That worked out nicely.

"We can do push-ups and sit-ups," I brag.

"Really?" I nod in confirmation.

"I'll show you when we get home and if you say please I'll even do it without my shirt on."

"Are you a stripper? I mean for real? Is that how you earn your money?"

"Very funny," I say drily.

Ginny plays with Tramp as we head home. He finds a stick—a tree trunk really—and he's happy. Ginny chases after him and he clearly loves it. I'd love it too if it was me, she was chasing.

"Jump," she shouts happily—and he does. He really does. The fucker takes off and jumps over the park bench with the tree trunk in his mouth like it weighs nothing and like the bench is two inches high. Suddenly, I feel like such an idiot—again—for lifting him onto the vet's table. Dogs can do that to you.

I persuade Tramp to leave the tree trunk in the park and he reluctantly does. I've learned my lesson. Only once have I allowed him to bring one home and he demolished it in the living room like he was a beaver cutting down a tree. I might want to consider beaver in his mixed gene pool as well.

I'm happy about my forced minimalism when I open the door to my apartment. Despite my general dislike of cleaning, I vacuum frequently because Tramp sheds. Of course, he does. Yet another thing to annoy me.

"So, what can I get you for breakfast?"

"Just coffee really."

"Don't trust my cooking?"

"Don't trust much of you at all."

"That's probably wise," I admit.

Tramp is right behind me when I go into the kitchen. He does this almost without fail every time we come home because he knows he will get a treat. That tradition started when he grew *very* large and every time, we came home from a walk I felt I had to reward him because he hadn't eaten anything he was not supposed to. He now sits down behind me as I open the cupboard and he's eyes are locked to every movement I make like he's considering a career in surveillance. I give him his treat and send him to his large and ridiculously expensive orthopaedic bed before I make coffee.

It's strange having Ginny in my kitchen and I have to admit it's not only when I'm in the bed or on the shower I'm thinking about her. In my dreams, she's been in my kitchen too. Usually, it's the morning after, she's wearing one of my dress shirts and we enjoy the bliss after a long night of lovemaking. Sigh.

"Are you alright?" Ginny asks and tears me out of my daydreaming.

"Do you want milk in your coffee?"

"Is that what you were thinking about? You looked almost dazed." I smile, but I don't answer her. I'm not admitting anything—not even to myself.

"Milk?" I ask and Ginny nods. I open the fridge and hand it to her. She pours and hands it back to me with a suspicious look on her face. I ignore it and close the fridge. I ignore it and pour the coffee. I ignore it, and hand her a mug.

"Thank you."

"Let's go sit down in the living room." That's not going to help me at all, because I've imagined her there too. On her knees in front of me and me sitting in the couch feeling like the king of the world in a far better way than DiCaprio did in 'Titanic.' That movie is from 1997 by the way. It was nominated for fourteen Oscars out of seventeen available, and won eleven.

Ginny looks around when she enters the living room. She's clearly surprised at the spartan look of the room and honestly, it looks like someone has just moved in and haven't finished decorating. She sits on one end of the couch, and I sit at the other. It's not saying much because it's rather small but at least I can pretend I'm polite. She has no idea what the two of us have done on this couch in my dreams. If she did know she probably wouldn't come anywhere near it.

"Uhm, you look like you need some furniture," Ginny says tentatively like she's not certain if I'm going to be offended or hurt because I'm actually a poor person.

"This is forced minimalism," I say and shrug. "It's very trendy with people who have dogs the size of a pony," I say easily, and Ginny quirks an eyebrow.

"So, it's Tramp's fault?"

"As always. Here, I'll show you," I say and put my coffee on the table. I pull out my phone and open the picture folder labelled 'Tramp.' Yes, like any other insane dog owner I have an entire *folder*—filled to the brim—with photos of my dog. I scroll until I find the photo of Tramp wearing the side table and then I move closer to Ginny so she can see the photo. I could just have handed her the phone, but that's would just be dumb when this gives me the perfect excuse to be closer to her. Ginny laughs when she sees the photo.

"That's so sad."

"I considered taking him to the dog park like that," I disclose.

"Brave," Ginny acknowledges, and nods.

"Not really. I didn't do it."

"Then you're smarter than you look."

"Exceedingly sexy doesn't rule out smart, you know?" Ginny just snorts and rolls her eyes. I'm still right, though.

"Do you have more photos?"

"I'm a dog owner, what do you think?"

"I think your phone is running out of disk space." She's right about that.

I show her photos of Tramp balancing all sort of things on his nose. I've also caught him mid sneeze and sleeping on his back with his tongue sticking out. He hardly looks like a dog on those. There's a photo of him tumbling into his ridiculously large and expensive orthopaedic bed because he stepped on the rope he was carrying. Chasing his tail—a classic—and barking at the mirror. I wish I'd videoed that one.

Ginny laughs until her eyes water, I do too and then I suddenly realise how close I am to her. My stomach clenches in an unknown feeling of anticipation. It feels like I've been waiting for this for a long, long time. I lean in to kiss her, but then I hesitate. There's no noise from the hallway, and I haven't even given Tramp a chew bone. There's no sound of paws, no sound of disasters of any kind. No whining, no howling—he's so quiet right now I'm not even sure he's breathing. That part shouldn't bother me, though.

"What?" Ginny asks quietly.

"I don't hear anything," I say and slowly pull away from her.

"What are you talking about?" I don't answer, I get up from the couch and walk into the hallway. Tramp is on his large and ridiculously expensive orthopaedic bed, and he raises his head to look at me. He's wagging his tail as I squat and pet his head. He licks my arm and I'm feeling confused.

"Why are you not making any noise?" I ask. He wags his tail and groans and digs his back further into his ridiculously large and expensive orthopaedic bed in order to get even more comfortable. He seems all right, he doesn't look like he just had some sort of stroke, or is broken in any way, and I have absolutely no idea what's going on right now.

I sit there for a while and pet him carefully almost like I'm expecting him to die any moment. He doesn't. I don't understand what's going on. Not with Tramp, not with the feeling in the pit of my stomach. Ginny comes into the hallway, she's brought her jacket, and I know what that means even before she says anything.

"I think I'd better go," she says quietly.

"What? No, don't go." I stand up.

"I don't think Tramp's the cockblocker, Simon."

"Usually he is." I don't want her to leave, but right now I'm so confused about Tramp's behaviour. The door closes behind Ginny, and I look at Tramp. What the hell is going on?

At first, I'm a bit annoyed Ginny has left, but then it dawns on me. Tramp's done acting up when I bring a woman home. I'm getting laid within days and I'm a fucking happy man. Until I'm not.

Friday night on my couch, I've only just kissed June and taken her dress off when she suddenly stiffens.

"What's he doing?" She whispers.

"What?" I'm so fucking turned on I'm almost dazed and it takes me a moment to focus. Until a moment ago, I was sucking her nipples and she was grinding her pussy against my cock, and I was feeling pretty God damn happy. I turn my head and come face to face with Tramp who's sitting at the end of the couch staring at us.

"Bed," I say. He yawns demonstratively and exposes a terrifying mouth filled with dangerous-looking teeth and June scrambles off my lap in fear. He's only about two feet away, so if he was going for the Jaws effect, he totally nailed it. Again. Fucker. Maybe he's part shark too? "Simon says bed," I growl, and he reluctantly retreats into the hallway.

"Wow, you're so commandeering," June says breathlessly.

"Where were we?" I say smiling as I look at her.

"You were just about to get lucky." Thank fuck. She unbuttons my jeans, and my cock practically jumps into her hand. "Love you're not wearing underwear," she says just before she lets herself slide to the floor, so she can suck on my cock. I groan happily because this feels so fucking good. She's sucking the head and jerking me off at the same time and right now I'm considering proposing to her.

"That's amazing," I moan. I clench my ass, if I don't I think I might either come or push my cock down her throat. Not sure she's up for either after only three minutes with my jeans off. Besides, with a cock the size of mine you have to be careful—for both our sakes. "Oh yeah," I moan as she grabs my balls and sucks my cock slightly deeper into her mouth. God, I've missed this too. I definitely need a woman to worship my cock more often. "Getting close," I warn her because I really am. Just one more…June lets out a shriek and scrambles to her feet and leaves me and my cock in total confusion. Tramp whimpers like his dog hearing just got fried by the shrill sound. He bumps into the large armchair and pushes it into the wall with a massive thud. When June lets out another squeak, he barks. Not threateningly, but like he thinks he's just found a new play person. Fuck off Tramp, she's *my* play person.

"He just licked my back," she says panicky. She's only wearing a tiny thong so she's God damn lucky that was the only thing he licked. I don't tell her that though.

"No harm done, right?" I ask.

She looks hesitant.

I smile. Indulgently, persuasively—I hope.

She smiles a little too.

Then she looks at Tramp.

He starts humping the corner of the couch.

She practically sprints out the door.

"What the fuck are you doing to me?" I snarl at Tramp.

Blank stare.

"You did that on purpose."

Tail twitches.

"Why would you do that?"

Tapdancing.

"Why can't I have a little fun?" I groan and rub my face. Control. I need control over my life.

*

Saturday night, I shower, I put on enough cologne to make Tramp sneeze and paw his snout when he comes into the bathroom to watch me—and probably look for a way to sabotage my plans. That'll teach him.

"You're on your own," I tell him. "I need to get laid. Don't wait up."

I tell a woman called Cate I'd rather deal with her jealous ex-boyfriend if he stops by—he's a heavyweight wrestler by the way—than I want to bring her home to Tramp. This earns me a lot of admiration—simply for being stupid—and I lap it up. I'm starting to feel like Winnie the Pooh who will do all sort of stupid things to get to the honey. Cate's got flaming red hair, green eyes—just like Ginny—and long claw-like nails that are painted black. I'm going to get hurt—hopefully by her and not her ex-boyfriend—and I can't wait. She has already ripped my shirt and licked my chest before she even brings me home.

She demands I spoil her and I'm looking forward to it. I'm kissing my way up her leg towards her honeypot—call me Winnie—when my phone rings. I ignore it.

"Your phone's ringing," she points out breathlessly.

"Ignore it," I pant. She does, but it keeps ringing and keeps ringing and in the end I'm the one who can't ignore it. And I haven't even tasted her honey yet.

"What?" I snarl without even looking at the caller ID.

"Simon, I'm very worried about your dog," my neighbour, Mr Roberts, says. In the background, I hear a moaning sound like someone's slowly killing a harmonica. Slowly torturing it actually. Slowly, painfully torturing rather—you get the idea.

It only takes me ten minutes to get dressed and sprint home like my life depends upon it. As soon as I get of the elevator on my floor, I hear the loudest, most insane moaning, whining, awoo-o-o-o-sound I've ever heard—it sounds even worse than on the phone. Mr Roberts is standing in the hallway wringing his hands nervously and I sprint towards him as I fumble to get my keys out of my pocket. The moment I put the key in the lock, everything turns quiet—except for the resonance that's making my ears hurt.

I open the door and look inside. The apartment looks like a war zone. By the looks of it, I have nothing left in my apartment to wipe my ass. Tramp has ripped so much toilet paper apart it looks like it's been snowing. The paper was located on the top shelf of the bathroom closet. I also see the toilet brush and I almost want to throw up thinking about him swinging it wildly, spraying water everywhere in the living room.

"Someone had fun," Mr Roberts says beside me, and he sounds impressed.

"Yeah, thanks for calling," I say drily.

I close the front door and slowly walk into what doesn't look like my apartment anymore. God damn it! The tall kitchen cupboard is open—I have absolutely no idea how he did this. The spaghettis are no more, there's flour all over the floor, making it look like a coke lab exploded in my kitchen. Thank God nobody called the police when he was making a racket.

"What the hell…" I have no words for the mess in my apartment. By the looks of it, he rolled in the flour and there're huge white paw prints all over the place. All over, I shite you not. And he's been licking the TV again, with flour on his face. You've got to take a moment to appreciate the work Tramp's put into this.

I hardly know where to begin, but still, I start by gathering ripped paper in a plastic bag. Tramp looks at me like he's interested in what I'm doing and like it's totally unrelated to him.

"I hate you," I tell him.

Innocent look.

"If you keep that up, we won't have a home."

Frown.

"I'm serious."

Roll of eyes.

"We'll live in the…"

Ears perk—probably expecting me to say park.

"Street."

Disappointment.

"I'll lose my job."

Wagging of tail.

"That means no bed."

Shrug.

"That means no food."

A look of true horror.

A Lot of Teeth

Fun fact: Dental sticks are a waste. No matter how large, they're bitten in half and swallowed and no way in hell does that count as any kind of toothbrushing. Fuck you very much for that suggestion, vet. Ka-ching.

You live and you learn right? I hope so. Every cupboard the apartment now has a child safety lock on it. They're not expensive—until you buy about a hundred of them. If Tramp wants to open the cupboards, he'll have to eat his way through. I wouldn't put it past him, but I have yet to come up with a plan to prevent that from happening. I'm not pulling his teeth out no matter how tempted I was that night he ruined my time with Cate.

Margot must be the bravest woman in the world, because she has agreed to watch Tramp for once. I have a two-day workshop at work and come hell or high water I can't miss it. If I do, I might actually get fired and that—as you know—means no food for Tramp.

Tramp is fascinated with their baby despite they called the poor thing Edmund. Tramp lays his enormous head by the baby's side and the baby pulls his fur and pokes his eyes and squeals delighted. We've got a torturer on our hands, and I support his career wholeheartedly as long as it's Tramp, who's the victim. Margot frowned a bit the first hundred times Tramp laid his dirty chin on the baby's white bedsheets, now she's just given up—and don't I know that feeling. But Tramp protects the baby with the ugly name and that has earned Margot's forgiveness. Now, she thinks it's cute. Yeah right.

On day two when the workshop has finished, I've just parked my car in front of my sister's house when I see a man by her front door. He's young, has blond hair, and wearing a suit that looks slightly too big. His posture is rigid and a bit aggressive and he looks out of place somehow.

"I'm not interested," Margot snaps and attempts to close the door. I say attempt because the idiot—whoever he is—puts his foot in the door. I'm going to kick his ass. I don't have the time, because Margot lets out a startled shriek, the baby starts crying, and I hear a Godawful growling bark from inside the house.

And that's when things get out of hand.

Margot opens the door to slam it hard, but this time it's Tramp that's in her way—or rather his teeth. The only thing visible from this side of the front door is his mouth and teeth that's snapping wildly. There's froth around his mouth and the clacking sound of his jaws almost drowns out the snarling. He's snapping the air in blind fury, and I've got to admire Margot for being able to keep him in. Right now, she's probably—for once—happy her ass is still as big as it was when she was pregnant. Rhino size.

I jump the garden gate and sprint towards the man who's either frozen in fear or too stupid to move, because he's still standing a few feet from the door, and he must be able to feel the warm breath from Tramp's snapping jaws.

"Tramp, enough," I shout. His snarl decreases, but I still hear him growling.

"Simon?" Margot asks.

"Close the door, Margot. Go inside," I demand. I have absolutely no idea what Tramp would do if he got out right now. Maybe he'd just be happy to see me, maybe he'd rip the strange man apart in the middle of Margot's neat garden path—and then I'd be in real trouble. Thankfully, Margot manages to close the door and I look at the man in front of me. He's panting in fear, a few Watchtower magazines are spread on the garden path, and he's desperately hugging Awake! for comfort. Tramp eats paper too, just so you know, and I'm pretty sure not even God himself could safe this guy if Tramp had gotten lose.

"Are you insane?" I yell.

"G-god provides me with the c-courage I need," he stutters and pretends he's not shaking like a leaf at this test God just put in front of him.

"He'd better provide you with an ambulance if that dog had gotten lose." He hurries away and I clearly see his pants are wet. For his sake, I hope God will provide him with another pair of pants as well.

*

I've never understood how Tramp was able to eat canned dog food. I've never understood how he could find the smell appetising either, but I'm in for yet another lesson courtesy of Tramp. Park equals geese. Geese equals droppings. Dropping equals…You know where this is going, right? Tramp has started to eat goose droppings, and if I thought canned dog food was bad, I had another thing coming. I don't smell the droppings, but just seeing Tramp's mouth and teeth smeared with shite…I almost throw up.

At home, I drag him to the bathroom and into the shower stall. He's somewhat confused about this, but he doesn't resist until I turn on the water and point the shower head straight into his mouth. He flinches and accidentally pushes the shower head thereby changing the spray to high pressure massage. He snarls and bites the water. His jaws snap like it's another Jehovah's Witness and I only just manage to keep him at a distance. I've got one hand at his collar, I'm holding the shower head with the other, and thank fuck I've been pulling his blasted rope so much, because I actually have the strength to hold him. Barely.

"Stop it."

Snarl.

"You've got shit in your mouth, idiot."

Snap, snap, snap.

"Stop it, Tramp."

Bark, snarl, snap, snap, snap.

"Enough!"

Growl.

"Simon says no!"

Snap, snap, snap.

See? Told you "Simon says" would only work a few precious times.

One good thing has come of Tramp's furious attack on the water—his mouth is now clean. The downside—because there's always a downside when it comes to Tramp—there's water all over the bathroom. All over. The shower curtain was ripped off the rail within moments and now everything is drenched. Everything. Every towel in sight. Every comic I read when I take a shite. The bathmat is floating under the sink cabinet. Yes, floating.

The battle with Tramp has lasted half an hour and I exhausted sink to the floor of the shower stall with a groan. I wrap the shower head in the ruined shower curtain, so Tramp won't see it and attack it again. He's drenched too and stands right in front of me when he shakes every bloody drop of water from his fur. Every drop. Several times. I don't even attempt to shield myself. The bathroom smells of wet dog and if you don't know it then you can put it on the list of bad smells. Believe me. Now that's Tramp has shaken himself off in front of me he seems happier, and he wags his tail when he looks at me like he's waiting for the next thing to entertain him.

Do you know the movie 'Singin in the Rain' from 1952? It's a musical romantic comedy directed and choreographed by Gene Kelly—of course—and Stanley Donen. It's starring Gene Kelly—of course—Donald O'Connor, and Debbie Reynolds and featuring Jean Hagen, Millard Mitchell and Cyd Charisse. One of the most memorable—if not *the* most memorable—scene from the movie is Gene Kelly dancing and singing in the rain. Why am I thinking about this now? Because Tramp is tapdancing in the large puddle that is my bathroom floor like he's auditioning for the theatrical version. The bathmat has a sound of its own and makes his repertoire sound far more extensive than it is. So, my dog now eats goose droppings and attacks water. And he wants to be the next Gene Kelly.

I talk to the vet about the goose droppings. He rules out parasites and other physical reasons—meaning it's probably mentally. I believe it! Tramp shows no other signs of anxiety, his noise-making is probably attention-seeking because I'm his only human. I can't believe I've paid money for someone else to tell me this. Ka-ching.

I'm in over my head, and I don't know what to do about it. I'm *never* admitting it out loud, but I love Tramp. But I have to work and loving him doesn't mean I should never be able to bring a woman home. A man has got to eat and sleep. And he has to fuck if he's to keep his sanity. That Maslow guy had the idea when he put sex among the most basic physiological needs. Something tells me, I'll need a new pair of striped pj bottoms for when I go to the asylum.

*

I haven't seen Ginny in the park for a while, but it makes sense. It's September and the sun doesn't get up until almost seven. I miss her though. Not that I'm admitting that out loud either.

I've changed the routine of our evening walk. We go to the park, but on the way home we walk through the city. Tramp is very interested in the train, and for a moment I consider taking him. Just to try it out. He must be leashed, and station staff can refuse entry if your dog is misbehaving. Meaning we probably won't be allowed to board the train. So, I *walk* through the city alone. With my dog. I don't mind being single at all, but I mind my sex-life is practically gone because my life is dictated by a furry cockblocker.

Tramp knows the noises of the city, he's unfazed by strangers, so I'm surprised when he one night suddenly lets out snarling bark similar to the one, he made when facing the

Indominus Rex on the telly. Only now he's a grown dog and not a large puppy. Come to think of it, this sounds like when he was protecting Margot from the Jehovah's Witness. My dog is probably an atheist. Or the Antichrist—more plausible that one.

I can practically hear the rumbling starting in his barrel-sized chest—a dire wolf is definitely a pussy. Jesus, he's intimidating and I'm actually too surprised to say anything until he barks again. The couple in front of us stops and slowly turns around. My heart stutters at the sight of Ginny. She's holding hands with a man and already I hate the fucker. Guess she's not a lesbian after all, and I feel like I've been punched in the stomach.

"Sit," I command, and Tramp slams his bum down on the pavement. He's still baring his teeth and his hackles are standing straight up like he's turned punker in seconds—all he needs is a dash of pink. His body is trembling and he's ready to strike.

"Illegal," I say. That has become the new 'bad word.'

Snarl decreasing.

"Hey, boy," Ginny says softly, and Tramp stops snarling completely. His teeth are still bared but I see his tail twitching. "You've been a good boy?" She asks in a musically voice and Tramp can't help himself. His tail starts wagging and his huge body is joining in as he whines delighted.

"Ginny do you really think…" the man beside her asks. The moment the man steps forward and reaches for Ginny, Tramp lets out a series of snarling barks. There's no doubt in my mind he's warning this guy off. Good boy—I don't like him either. Tramp still hasn't taken his furry bum of the pavement and I'm having mixed emotions. My dog is a terrifying beast, but he listens to me. I think I might be proud again. The man quickly retreats, but Ginny stays where she is. She's wearing a dark purple dress under her coat. No cleavage, but she still looks like the perfect wet dream to me.

"Miss me?" She coos, and Tramp gets up, wagging his entire body enthusiastically. He slams his hip against my leg, and I take a step to the side to keep my balance.

"I think that's safe to say." Ginny looks at me and smiles. Little does she know Tramp's not the only one who has missed her.

"Haven't you found other people to yell at in the park?"

"You're my favourite," I say softly. I feel equally happy to see her and sad she's with another. And I want to hurt the man she's with. If I were a dog, I'd have only two of those feelings to deal with.

"Should I be flattered?" She asks grinning while she's petting Tramp. He has thrown his enormous body on the pavement and rolled onto his back so Ginny can pet him. Selfish bastard, but I don't blame him one bit.

"Definitely," I say seriously. She really is one of my favourite persons—and not only, to yell at.

"Ginny," the man says carefully, and Tramp glances his way, giving him the evil eye. The man doesn't step any closer, but sadly Ginny gets up. She hugs me briefly and that's about the best thing that has happened to me for as long as I can remember.

"What kind of an idiot calls his dog Tramp?" The man scoffs as they walk away.

"He named himself," Ginny says, and I can hear her laughing. God, I miss her laugh too.

Unexpected Visitor

Fun fact: Dogging is slang for the act of having sex in public while people watch.

It's the beginning of November and it's been almost a month since I saw Ginny *that* night with *that* man. I often regret I didn't knock him out, dragged him into an alley, and let Tramp eat him. I would have saved a lot of money on dog food too. I miss her in the park—once I avoided her, now I'm looking for her. I know it's no use, but I can't seem to help myself.

Autumn and winter mornings are a dog owner's nightmare—at least it is for me—even if it is Sunday and Tramp has managed to control himself until seven. The sun has barely risen, but at least it's bright enough to see. Barely. I should have brought a flashlight.

I'm wearing boots, pj, a scarf, a hoodie, and a jacket. I forgot the beanie. Only good thing is that it's not as early, as usual. When mornings grew darker, I refused to let Tramp pull me all the way to the park. If he needed to piss, he could do it round the corner, molesting a lamp post, because I'm not running around in the darkness of the park with a flashlight, because he thinks it's funny. Remember I told you I've got a really smart dog? It's true, because Tramp has already learned that if he pulls my ass out of bed before daybreak, we're *not* going to the park. That only happens later when the sun has actually risen. This time of year, it's a good thing, but already I dread the coming summer, where sunrise is practically in the middle of the night. Yes, to me a quarter to five in the morning is in the middle of the night.

Today, it only takes about half a second of me not paying attention…and he's off. Shite, I thought we'd gotten past this. Apparently not and one day, I may lose my dog because we've gradually broken every sodding park law there is. He's not in sight, he doesn't respect wildlife, and it was impossible for me to clean up after him the day he had diarrhoea. He's barked at Ginny, so he's not exactly kept the place safe and pleasant. At home, he's been a noisy nuisance to the neighbours—even if I haven't had any complaints—and when we met Ginny and her date, it was pretty clear he's dangerous. I've done my best, I really have, and the thought of losing him is guts me. In a rare moment of clarity, I see all my savings—what's left of them anyway—fly out the window for a dog behaviourist. I'll never get a house and garden for him if he keeps spending my money on other things.

"Tramp!" I yell, but he's running like crazy, and I can help being amazed. The length of his strides is huge, the aerial phase insane, and I'm wondering whether he's part greyhound too. I'll need my car—or a F1—to catch him, but I still run after him, yelling his name. Dog owners really are crazy.

He's stopped at a bench about a quarter of a mile down the path by the lake. He's got his enormous head in a woman's lap and my heart starts pounding…until she gently pats his head. I have no idea who this woman is, but she's got some balls petting a monster like that alone in the park. It's only when I come closer, I recognise Ginny. She looks so frail somehow and not quite like herself.

"I should've listened to you," she coos, and hugs Tramp just as I make it to the bench. She looks up at me and she looks heartbreakingly sad.

Do you know there are different kind of tears? And I'm not talking about how they look under a microscope. When men cry, we usually look manly as hell doing it. You know—dignified, stoic, tough, all the while our eyes are leaking. When children cry, it's often extremely noisy and accompanied by snot and saliva. It's disgusting. When women cry, it's hysterical and irrational. It's annoying. But in Ginny's case the crying is quiet and heart-breaking. Tears tickle down her cheeks and her nose is a little red.

"Hey, drunk Potter girlfriend," I say quietly.

"Hey, asshole." She smiles slightly as she lets go of Tramp who whimpers like he hasn't had enough hugs.

"He's the asshole," I say and point to Tramp. "An ugly one to boot."

Roll of eyes.

"He's good-looking."

Smirk.

"You're kidding me?"

"No. He's gorgeous in the manly way, like scruff."

Puffs out chest, raises head proudly.

I run my hand over my scruff and Ginny rolls her eyes at me.

"No, I'm not complimenting your lack of shaving."

"Why not? I look hot like this."

"So, you say."

"Come on, Gin. You think I look hot." She quirks an eyebrow. "Sexy too," I insist. "I have witnesses, you know?"

"Only to the fact that your cock is huge, and you have a great ass."

"True," I say and sit down next to her with an exaggerated sigh. Tramp lays down like he knows we're going to be here for a while. And we are. For as long as she wants to.

"I'm going home," she says quietly.

"Let us walk you."

"To my house."

"For today?"

"Permanently." I feel slightly panicked and Tramp whimpers loudly like he too is panicking about Ginny leaving town forever.

"Why?"

"I lost my job." She shakes her head. "So stupid." Tears run down her cheeks, but she looks more regretful than sad. I reach out for her and gently hug her. God, she smells good. And she feels so good too. Nothing has ever felt this good. I want to fuck her so bad. I want to hold on to that gorgeous ass as she rides my cock. Slowly, leisurely, torturing me with her wet pussy, soft skin, and the sight of her tits hovering over me.

"What's stupid about it?" I ask carefully.

"The man I was with that night…"

"The one Tramp didn't like?" She nods and smiles slightly.

"He asked me out, said it didn't matter we worked together."

"But?"

"It did matter when I wouldn't sleep with him or let him take credit for my ideas."

"I should've let Tramp take his balls of that night."

"Agreed."

"He was the head of my department." I don't like where this is going at all.

"He was the one who fired you?" I ask and she nods slowly.

"I just threw everything away."

"I'm sorry, Gin."

"Yeah." She just shrugs and I wish there was something I could do to make her feel better. Tramp has placed his massive head on her feet—I hope this means he's comforting her and not just using her for a pillow. She sighs. "I'm so pissed."

"Yeah, you want to punch something?"

"Are you offering?" She asks tiredly.

"Not really," I admit.

"It's okay. Besides, I already did." She holds up her hands and I see small bruises on her knuckles.

"Did you punch him?" I ask impressed, but Ginny shakes her head.

"Punched a hole in his door. He looked rather spooked."

"Good girl," I praise with the same tone of voice I use when I try to convince myself Tramp is s good boy. He's not. Really.

"It was only cardboard, but it felt *so* good." Jesus, the way she said that—*felt so good*—makes my cock twitch in appreciation because it doesn't understand what the rest of this conversation is all about. I clear my throat.

"How about some coffee? I'm freezing my balls of."

"Still no underwear?"

"Looking at me you know it."

"But it would have kept your balls warm."

"You're up for the job?" I don't like seeing Ginny sad, I like feisty Ginny much better, and I'll gladly provoke her if that's what it takes.

"And he's back," she says and rolls her eyes.

"I still haven't gotten any better at this early morning shite."

"It's hardly early, Simon."

"It is to me."

"Well, at least you're now showing me your ass."

"Give me time." As I stand up, I reach back and tear the fabric of my pj, exposing my ass. "See?" I say and thank fuck Ginny bursts out laughing. I might be freezing my ass off, but I don't give a shite as long as she looks happy. That might change if I get arrested.

We walk side by side through the park and Tramp walks besides me like this is where he's supposed to be. It *is* where he's supposed to be, only sometimes he forgets. Honestly, he forgets often.

"You've done good with him," Ginny says and nods at Tramp.

"Really?" She nods and I feel a burst of pride.

"I don't think many dog owners could've commanded their dog to stay put when we met you that night." I absently pat Tramps head, because I feel so fucking relieved. Maybe I'm not, as bad as I think. I hope I'm not.

"Couldn't command him to do shite today. He just took off."

"He came running straight to me."

"So, it's your fault? I'll take it."

"Knew you would."

Ginny entertains herself and Tramp on the way back to my apartment by making him jump over pretty much everything we see. He sits, he lays down, he stays, he blindly does everything she says, and he looks like he's having a good time doing it too. The traitor worships Ginny and hangs on her every word—or maybe he just wants her to be happy too. He seems to like her and listen to her, so when we get to the road, I just hand her the leash. She's a natural with Tramp—I guess he likes foxes too.

I'm really freezing my ass off by the time we get to my apartment. I try to stay manly and unaffected, but my teeth are practically clattering and I'm shivering like a small dog on a thin leash. Ginny doesn't say anything, and my not so fragile ego appreciates this.

Tramp leads the way up the stairs as always and he also sits down in front of the door, waiting for me to unlock it. Inside the apartment he will—on a good day—dash to his ridiculously large and expensive orthopaedic bed and wait for his treat. He often rolls his eyes at the slowest dog owner in the world.

I face the front door to unlock it, and only a second later, I hear Samuel's door open across the hall. Great, I'm showing him my ass because I wanted to make Ginny laugh. Now I'm not sure it's worth it.

"Hi, Simon," he says breathlessly. I grunt, but I don't answer, and I don't turn around.

"I'm, Ginny," she says behind me.

"I'm, Samuel," he breathes and I'm pretty sure he's not panting because of Ginny. "You know, Simon?" He practically moans, and I only hope he doesn't ask her if he can watch us fuck.

"We're friends."

"Only friends, that's great," he pants. He almost sounds like he's run a marathon.

"Good friends," Ginny says delighted and smacks my ass. I hear a sharp intake of breath—I don't want to think about it. But I really want to think about her spanking me. Or not. It'll give me a hard-on. Samuel will see. I *don't* want to think about it.

"Come on," I say and quickly push Ginny through my front door. Tramp is already inside and he's sitting in the hallway waiting for a treat. I slam the door behind me.

"What's wrong?" Ginny asks and she looks like she's about to burst out laughing.

"I take it back. Tramp's not the asshole, you are. Do you have any idea what you've done?"

"I think so. That nasty little man got an instant hard-on watching your ass."

"I'm never cheering you up again," I groan and Ginny laughs.

"I'm…nah…I'm not even sorry," she's still laughing, and I'm still in some sort of pain. "You've got a great ass."

"Not helping, you're still a bitch," I pout.

"But I really needed the cheering up." She looks at me and smiles. "Thank you."

"You're an asshole," I shout as I head towards the bedroom. I need clothing unless Ginny wants to strip and come with me. "Give Tramp his treat, it's in the cupboard next to the sink."

"Then will you forgive me?"

"No and I don't want to forgive you just because you smile at me either," I complain.

"I'll make coffee," she yells back, and I swear I can hear in the tone of her voice she's smiling.

"Now, I love you," I yell. "Even more if you come to my bedroom and make amends." Please come to the bedroom and make amends—such a nice dream. She doesn't answer, but I hear her laughing.

In my bedroom, I turn and look at the mirror and groan—that's a lot of my ass on display! Don't do it…don't think about what Samuel is doing right now. Tramp comes into the bedroom and for a tiny second, I hoped it was Ginny.

"You need to snarl every time you see Samuel," I say and shudder.

Blank stare.

"I take care of you; you should take care of me too."

Cock of head. Might consider it.

"You'll regret it if Samuel kidnaps me one day."

Narrows eyes and lip twitching.

"He'd keep me, you know? Do horrible things to me."

Growling.

"That's it. Good boy."

What the fuck?

"Samuel."

Tentative snarl.

"Goooood boy. Samuel."

Snarl.

"Goooood boy. Suck a gooood boy," I coo. "Samuel."

Evil snarl.

I pat him on the head, and he wags happily—he's looking for a bribe, so I'd better get dressed and give him his treat. I really want him working with me on this.

Do you know that old Gene Wilder movie 'Young Frankenstein' from 1974? It's also starring Marty Feldman and it was directed by Mel Brooks. The horses whinny every time then housekeepers name is mentioned. Fun fact: her name is Frau Blücher, and blücher means glue in German, and I'm certain the horses think they're headed straight for the glue factory whenever she's nearby. If I can just get a Frau Blücher-principle going and I can make Tramp snarl every time I say Samuel, I'll be really pleased. Hope it doesn't come back to bite me in the ass.

I put on a pair of track pants and a sweater. Then I pull off the sweater and put on a hoodie and only zips it halfway. Then I pull off the hoodie and put on a tight T-shirt. Much better. Only I'm freezing, so I put the hoodie back on, but I don't zip it. I look in the mirror and determine I look pretty good—you know, manly and muscular and all. I hope Ginny likes it. And then I ruin the manly look by putting on purple knitted wool socks my mother has made for me because I'm often cold in the park. Not that I remember putting them on when I'm half awake and tumbling out the door at shite o'clock in the morning.

"What were you two doing in there?" Ginny asks as I re-enter the kitchen.

"Practicing snarling at Samuel."

"Useful."

"I think so," I say as I brush closely by her to open the cupboard. Tramp is right at my heels.

"Samuel," I say as I turn towards him and hold out the biscuit.

Blank stare.

"Samuel."

Eyes on biscuit.

"Samuel."

Whimper. Eyes on biscuit.

"Samuel."

Growl.

"Good boy. Samuel."

Bark.

"Samuel."

Bark, bark.

I groan and give him the biscuit. This is going to need a lot of work.

"Nice socks," Ginny comments.

"You would notice the socks, wouldn't you?"

"Well, you've stopped flashing your ass."

"I've got a great ass. It needs to be flashed one in a while. Anything else you want me to flash? Just ask."

"No, I'm good."

"I'm disappointed."

"Go flash your neighbour."

"Now you're just being evil."

When the coffee has finished brewing, we pour it, and go into the living room. We sit on the couch, and I try not to think about the last time we sat here. I almost kissed her.

"When are you moving?" I ask.

"This weekend. I just ned to pack a few things and rent a car."

"Let me drive you. I have a Range Rover and a tow bar."

"What about Tramp?"

"He can be home alone," I say.

Loud whimpering.

"We could also bring him," I suggest because I'm an idiot.

Wagging tail.

"He'd love it there," Ginny says.

Enthusiastic bark.

"Are you sure it's no trouble?" She asks tentatively.

Whimper and pleading look.

"Boxes in the back seat, no problem at all."

"And a tow bar?"

"Yeah, I'll tie Tramp to the tow bar and put your boxes in the cage."

Loud howling.

"Simon," Ginny chides and punches my arm. "He didn't mean it, Tramp," she says soothingly and pats Tramps head.

"Yeah, I did." I didn't.

Whining.

Ginny stands up.

"You are such an asshole," she says casually.

"An asshole with a car and a tow bar."

"I'll take it. See you Saturday." She kisses my cheek lightly and then takes her leave.

"Why do you always have to be the centre of attention?" I ask Tramp when we're alone.

Confused look.

"Ever consider I might want some time alone with Ginny?"

Roll of eyes.

"She likes me."

Groaning.

No way he's buying that. I'm not quite sure I do either, but I really hope she does.

Miss Marple Land

Fun fact: The fictional character Miss Marple features in 12 novels, and 20 short stories. The author Agatha Christie was a dog lover and owned many dogs throughout her lifetime, usually a terrier of some sort. She hated marmalade pudding and cockroaches.

Ginny was right, Tramp loves her home. The moment he's out of the car, he takes of running until Ginny let's out a shrill whistle any hooligan would envy her. I do too actually, and I think I'm going to complain to Matt—obviously he hasn't taught me to whistle properly.

"Tramp." Tramp immediately turns around and runs to her. "Here." She pats her leg, and he obeys faster than anything I've ever seen. Her voice is hard and commanding, and I swear my knees jerk to obey. I want to be a good boy, then maybe she'll pet me too. Tramp elegantly rounds her—the bastard doesn't even bump into her—and he sits down puffing out his chest. He's a proud fucker right now. I might be too. She praises him with her soft voice and pats his head. I scratch my chest because I'm almost desperate for the attention she's giving Tramp right now. She could give me a collar, call me a good boy, tie me up, and teach me any trick she wanted to, and I'd be game.

"Did you ever practice not to cross an invisible line?" She asks.

"Not for long, he just thought he was supposed to go through the rug." I'm very careful not to mention 'dig.' God only knows if he remembers the command and demolishes Ginny's garden.

"You got a bad word?"

"Try illegal."

"Illegal?" Tramp immediately cowers by Ginny's side. "That might work. What is it?" She asks.

"It's when I tell him he'll be taken away from me and put down, be banned from the park, or making us homeless because he can't behave, and I'll end up eating him because I'm starving." Tramp cowers at Ginny's side and the world's largest dog almost looks like he's trying to hide behind her. Apparently, he's not smart today.

"Wow, that's some narrative," she says baffled, and I shrug.

"It works."

"Okay."

Ginny and Tramp make their way round the huge garden and every time Tramp wants to explore the other side of the stone fence Ginny says illegal in a stern voice. It looks ridiculous, and she's closing in on dog owner insanity fast. It takes them about twenty minutes, and I just stand and watch them from a distance. She's fucking beautiful. And patient. With Tramp at least.

"He swims?" Ginny asks when she and Tramp returns from the round of the garden.

"Gladly. Particularly, if he can scare the shite out of geese and ducks."

"He'll probably be disappointed then, but I'd better get some towels. There's a pond-looking mudhole at the end of the garden."

Ginny shows me her garden. It's mostly withered but I can easily imagine it's nice in the summer. And contain about a thousand insects waiting to devour human flesh every chance they get. I'm good-looking and popular for sure, but I'm also convinced whenever I'm around insects with either stingers or mandibles, they gather in a circle and chant 'feast on his flesh,' like they're paying homage to the Witch King of Angmar. I spend most of my summers in a lemon-smelling cloud, hoping to keep insects away. Sometimes it's tough being this attractive.

There's a large area which is probably supposed to be a lawn, but it just looks like grass. Contrary to Ben and Margot's pristine garden, there're a lot of plants and flowers scattered all over like they've been allowed to grow wherever they wanted. I recognise lavender—only because Tramp usually pees on Margot's—but I have no idea what the rest of them are. There're a lot of trees and between two of them hangs a rope hammock.

"My favourite place," Ginny says when she notices I'm looking at the hammock.

"It's *November*," I point out.

"But the sun is shining and there're blankets."

"Let's try it out," I say because despite I'm always cold—and haven't brought my purple socks—the thought of laying in the hammock with Ginny sounds fantastic.

We bring a few boxes from the car and inside the house and Ginny goes looking for blankets and pillows. The house is cute, but at six-foot-four, I see it like a huge hazard for my head. I'm not even sure if this qualifies an actual house or just a cottage. The neighbour's house has half-timbering, and the garden is filled with withered hollyhocks. I noticed a pond by the church, and there were goats, sheep, and ducks in several gardens we drove by. If Miss Marple pops in for tea, I won't even be surprised. I hope she likes pony-sized dogs too.

I try to be casual—the manly way—about it, but I can hardly contain myself when Ginny returns with the blankets. We go to the garden, and I almost start tapdancing the way Tramp does, while she lays a blanket and a few pillows on the hammock and then gestures to me.

"Are you sure this is safe?" I tease and Ginny rolls her eyes.

"No, I hope you will entertain me like Donald Duck losing a battle to a folding chair." I send her a look of superiority and calmly sits down in the middle of the hammock before lying down. My male ego would've taken a deadly hit if I couldn't even lie down in a hammock. Yes, truly.

"You are so boring," Ginny says, and I have a moment of true fear when she practically jumps into the hammock beside me. She is not deterred by my no doubt, stricken look but pulls another blanket over us to make us warm and comfortable. The moment she lays down beside me, I feel *very* comfortable. I hug her close and she snuggles into me. Her tits are pressing against my chest, and I just barely manage to stop myself from kissing her hair and let my hand wander to her ass.

"We'd better stay close to keep warm," I say even if there's no way I'll be cold. Having Ginny this close to me is making my blood boil, it thunders in my entire body, my cheeks are warm, and my heart is pounding. Conclusion: I need a woman, not socks, to keep me warm.

"So sensitive," Ginny mocks.

"Only when it's worth my while."

"Snake."

"What?"

"Cold-blooded and sneaky." Oh well, can't really argue with that one.

"Don't take it personal if I get a hard-on," I say because that'll probably happen within a few seconds. Ginny just chuckles and I'm not sure if she knows I'm serious. She might find out though.

She lays down with her head on my shoulder and a hand on my chest. God, that feels good. My cock is stirring—fast—but she probably won't notice. My scrotum suddenly feels like it's already started the January diet and have forgotten to take my balls with it. Everything feels tight all of a sudden, and I wonder if I'm going to have a teenage-moment and come in my jeans. I succeed—barely—to relax. I look at the messy and withered garden and suddenly it's almost beautiful. I sigh contently and realise I feel happy and relaxed like I can't remember I've ever been. This is a strange and unknown feeling.

Tramp comes barging through the garden and he's looking as happy and dirty as I've ever seen him. I tense when he shows no signs of slowing down as he approaches. No no no no no no no no no, this is bad, this is very very bad, this is really bad…Tramp enthusiastically takes off from the ground and Ginny only have time to turn her head and exclaim, "Oh shit," before Tramps lands in the hammock with us. Ginny lets out a huff as the air is knocked out of her by a hundred fifty-pound dog. The hammock is swinging wildly, and I hear a loud cracking sound just before the hammock crashes to the ground. I land on top of Ginny, and she huffs as the air is knocked from her lungs. I slam my knees to the ground and tumble off Ginny, so I don't crush her. I need to get up fast, because I've got to stop Tramp. We're all more or less tangled in blankets and the hammock, I stumble as my foot is caught, and Tramp is panicking. He takes off, still tangled in the rope that used to hold the hammock and the huge branch is scrambling after him, increasing his panic.

The rope tightens as he gets further away, and his wild escape pulls the hammock from beneath my feet just as I've gotten up. I land on my back and the wind is knocked out of me. Ginny's still tangled in the hammock, and she lets out a surprised scream as Tramp pulls her across the large lawn with staggering speed. Winded, I'm crawling and almost running even before I get on my feet.

"Tramp, stop," I yell, still out of breath. But either he doesn't hear, is panicked, or just plain ignoring me, and he keeps going. Ginny manages to untangle herself from the hammock only a few feet before she would've hit an apple three. My heart is in my throat as she rolls a few times until she stills. Meanwhile, the hammock gets tangled in the apple three, I see the rope stretch and stretch…until it finally stops Tramp's rampage. He sits down on his ass, looking surprised like this has never ever happened to him before. I run to Ginny, who's just sat up, she's looking a bit dazed, and I'm worried.

"Ginny, are you alright?"

"What the hell just happened?" She asks.

"Welcome to the world of Tramp," I say drily.

"Wow, that was something…"

"Are you hurt?"

"A few bruises I think."

"I'll make a rug out of him," I growl. Tramp comes loping over despite my threat. He's tangled in the rope and the torn hammock, and the branch is hanging around his neck like some kind of trophy. It's huge, but he doesn't seem to notice. If he doesn't make it, as a rugby player when he grows up, he can definitely get a job as a tow truck.

I wish I could've stayed in the hammock with Ginny for hours. For that one moment, everything was perfect...And then that moment ended. I've stopped counting how many times Tramp has ruined a moment for me. Asshole.

Ginny makes dinner and orders Tramp out of the kitchen. In case you're wondering...there's no pleading puppy-dog eyes, no negotiation, no compromise. Ginny is the alpha bitch—no doubt about that. Besides, she has food. And bribe—or the possibility of it—works very well with dogs. While she cooks, he follows her every moment like he's a heat-seeking missile. He frowns when she puts dinner on the table, and he's sleeping soundly with half his front paws over the threshold to the kitchen—Ginny allows it—when we've finished eating. Of all the things I've probably done wrong raising Tramp, I've never ever fed him by the table. I can't stand it when you're having dinner and there's a dog sitting next to you with its mouth open, waiting for food and looking like a black hole.

We eat and talk and have coffee and talk some more. Midnight comes too fast, and I need to go home. It's a two-hour drive, and I already dread Tramp's morning walk. I wonder if you can get arrested for being a zombie. I think I might find out in the very near future. Tramp wakes up and wags his tail when I stand up and he looks at me like he's waiting for me to entertain him—and like he's going to make my life a living hell on the drive home. And tomorrow morning too, which incidentally—according to Tramp's internal clock—is about five hours away. Fucker.

"I'm going to miss you," I say solemnly as I hug Ginny by the front door. I wish I could kiss her. I wish I could cup those gorgeous tits and suck her nipples through her blouse. I wish I could squeeze her ass and press her against me. And strip her. And fuck her. And not get hurt. What a wonderful dream.

"Find someone else to yell at," she says with a smile that seems just a little bit sad. Or maybe I just wish it was.

"Can we come visit?" I ask.

"You want to?"

"We do." I don't want to go, and I want to kiss her. I end up doing neither, but I hug her goodbye for a long time—a horrible decision, really—and I have a hard-on all the way home. That hurts after two hours by the way.

Singing Chipmunks Can Drive You Insane

Fun fact: It is estimated about 200 million human couples in the world have sex every day, which means that roughly 60 million dogs are watching humans have sex on a daily basis.

Matt, Pete, Hugh, and Jeff come over Sunday afternoon for poker. Normally we meet on Saturdays because we're usually hung over the day after. I know I'm going to regret it tomorrow, because—you know—we're usually hungover. Tramp and I were home a little after two this morning, Tramp peed on a lamp post before we went up, but he still felt he needed to get out and pee—on the same bloody lamp post—at five thirty. He must hate me, he really must.

We' sit down by the dining room table and Tramp is pacified in his ridiculously large and expensive orthopaedic bed with a chew bone.

"What happened to you yesterday?" Jeff asks, while he's dealing cards.

"Helped Ginny. She's moved back to her house." To some ridiculous small village, I can't even remember what's called. I was pretty much in a daze when I drove home. I'll need her to text me the address when we're going to visit her.

"Have you fucked her yet?"

"For fuck's sake, Matt," Hugh exclaims and smacks him in the back of the head, like he isn't dying to know too.

"Well, did you?" Jeff asks.

"No," I say.

"Why the hell not?" Pete demands.

"We had a little bit of Tramp drama and hammock trouble."

"I sympathise," Jeff says.

"No balls got hurt in the process," I say.

"That came later. They must be blue by now," Matt says with a smirk. I've got nothing to say about that. The fucker is right, so I just punch him.

Hangover, not enough sleep for two nights in a row, and the absolute certainty we won't be meeting Ginny makes Monday lives up to its name as the most hated day of the week. Me and my hangover work from home today. Tramp seems slightly confused about this, but he 'only' spends half an hour staring at me like I'm an intruder before he shuffles off to his ridiculously large and expensive orthopaedic bed to nap and have his fun with the unicorn.

At three pm, Tramp wakes up. I hear him groan in the hallway, no doubt stretching in his ridiculously large and expensive orthopaedic bed. Then he comes to the dining room table, where I'm working, and stands beside me. I can *feel* him looking at me. I ignore him.

"I'm working."

Intensified staring.

"I'm *working*."

Pokes thigh with snout.

"I'm not coming home until four thirty, you know that."

Pushes arm with entire head.

Do you remember what I told about big dogs that whenever you think something is out of reach, it isn't? Tramp pushes his head under my elbow and then he slams his entire head down on the keyboard. The computer dings frantically, clearly it doesn't recognise this command. I recognise the command, because it means, "We're going to the park right now or else…"

*

Saturday morning, we go to the park and as soon as we get home, I wolf down my breakfast even faster than Tramp. He looks at me with a mix of admiration and wonder.

"We're going out today," I declare happily.

Wagging of tail.

"Do you know where we're going?"

Whimper.

"We're going to see Ginny."

Exited bark.

I'm excited too and I can hardly keep my foot of the speeder. Speed limits are going to be my worst enemy today—even worse than Tramp.

Twenty miles before we arrive at Ginny's, Tramp starts whimpering. Bee Gees is on the stereo, so Tramp should be happy. I ignore him for a few more minutes, but when he starts shuffling around in the cage too, I pull over and push the hazard lights. There's no way I'm risking anything in my car with a dog who pisses a lake. I open the boot and let Tramp jump out. He sniffs the grass at the roadside, but mostly he looks confused like he doesn't understand what we're doing. Suddenly, I don't either.

I drive the rest of the way to Ginny's house and the closer we get, the more Tramp whimpers. He shuffles around in his cage so much I feel it in the entire chassis of the car. He probably didn't need to piss twenty miles ago—he was just eager to get here. Apparently, my dog knows the way to Ginny better than I do. When I pull up in front of Ginny's house, he's in full Husky mode—meaning noisy like hell. The window in the back is slightly open, and I'm certain Ginny can hear his serenade from inside the house.

I grab the wine and the flowers from the front seat. I have an overnight bag on the backseat, but I'm not bringing it in—not at first at least. To keep them safe, I keep the flowers and the wine behind my back when I open the boot and the cage to Tramp's cage. He barges out and past me like a Greyhound taking off after a mechanical hare. Ginny has just exited the front door and he sprints to greet her.

When he reaches her, he doesn't barge into her—apparently, that's yet another difference between me and Ginny—but slows his pace, so he doesn't knock her over.

"There's my boy," she says and furiously rubs his sides. He whines delighted and glances at me like he wants to share his happiness with me. Or maybe he acknowledges I did good driving us here. Or maybe he's just gloating because he's the first one to great Ginny. It's probably the latter. I make my way up the path and when I reach them, he's still wagging his tail like crazy. I have to push my way past him to be able to reach Ginny. I kiss her cheek and hug her. God, she feels good.

"I've missed you," I say and kiss her cheek again. Tramp barges in between us and his entire body is *still* wagging madly, making both of us struggling to keep our balance. "*We've* missed you," I say and Tramp howls happily.

"So, it would seem," Ginny says and laughs. Despite Tramps jostling, she's still in my arms—barely—and that makes me almost as happy as Tramp is.

"Trust me."

"Did you bring your purple socks?" Ginny asks and I reluctantly let go of her.

"Should I have?"

"Are you up for a walk?"

"Of course." Mostly because I want to occupy Tramp. If I'm lucky, he'll even be tired tonight and sleep and leave me and Ginny alone.

If I were a man who believed in that sort of thing, I'd say the village and the surrounding area is therapeutic despite the vivid autumn colours have faded because *winter is coming*. I don't have to mention Game of Thrones, do I? I imagine this place will look like something out of a fairy tale book when it's covered in snow. Hills and moors and fields and drystone walls seem to be everywhere. In the distance, I see forests and steep hills. If I were a man who believed in that sort of thing, I'd let the rural beauty coax me into taking a deep breath of fresh air to feel better.

I put my arm around Ginny's shoulder as we walk across the field and fortunately, she doesn't seem to mind. It's comfortable walking beside her like this. The weather is cold but for once I'm not freezing, because I'm wearing my woollen socks—two pairs. Of course, I still look *terribly* masculine. Particularly since my mother grudgingly agreed to knit me some black and grey pairs—no stripes—so I can keep warm a little more discreetly.

"How's the cockblocker doing?" Ginny asks.

"A pro by now," I sigh. I'm twenty-seven and my sex-life was practically eliminated more than a year ago because of a sodding dog. Maybe it'd be fair to cut off his balls since he's pretty much castrated me. Come to think of it, I shouldn't feel guilty about considering it at all. Quite the contrary.

"You could leave him here for a weekend if you want to go out."

"Really?"

"I'd love to have him."

"Next week?"

"I'm staying in town next week, but I can dog-sit at your place if you don't need it?"

"That would be great."

"Just don't bring any of your conquests home," she says with a quirked eyebrow.

"Of course not, Tramp may ruin it despite you're there!" I say aghast. I can easily imagine it, and I wouldn't put it past Tramp to succeed.

Naturally, I'm a bit cold when we return to the house from out walk, but I pretend I'm not. Clearly my body temperature doesn't match my looks—you know *hot*. The house is nice and warm, and I pretend I'm only making fun when I stretch my feet towards the woodburning stove and complain about missing my purple socks. I'm not certain Ginny buys my nonchalance but thankfully, she lets me get away with it. You just got to love a woman like that.

I sit in the kitchen while she's making a late lunch for us. She's even provided me with a beer. It feels cosy sitting here and I almost manage to ignore the chair I'm sitting on is not only old and horrible, but terribly uncomfortable too. And it makes me restless.

Do you know the movie 'The Postman Always Rings Twice' from 1981? It's starring Jack Nicholson and Jessica Lange, and it's the fourth adaptation of the 1934 novel by James M Cain. I hardly remember the movie, it's been years since I saw it, and honestly, I only remember *one* scene from the entire movie. I don't have to tell which one, do I? It's the most controversial scene, the one on the kitchen table. Legend has it that the scene was so raw, so raucous, and so realistic that audiences thought it was real. I'd be up for a re-enactment right about now.

I desperately want to touch Ginny, which means I'm desperate to distract myself. I look around in the old kitchen which might have shitty chairs to sit on but has the same charm as the house does. There's a series of six abstract painting on the wall signed PM20. There's a lot of black, but also blue and green skies that look like they've cracked and are crying. Green and purple fields that are bleeding and pink and blue rivers that are burning. I should stop drinking now—really.

"Originals?" I ask, like I give a shite. Ginny nods.

"Do you know anything about art?"

"Not a thing."

"Me neither, but I couldn't help myself when I saw these." I look at them again and try to understand why. They're great, but erratic, and strangely depressing like the person who painted these had a really rough time. It's probably a dog owner. "I won three of them at work at the art lottery and then I bought the other three," Ginny tells me. I smile like I understand why she would do such a thing, but I honestly don't.

"How's the freelance business?" I ask.

"Slow. It takes a while building it up."

"Are you going to make it work?"

"I don't know," she says quietly. She sights and looks down. "My boss has told a lot of people in the business I'm a slut and they should only use me freelance if they're looking for a bad lay and a cheap concept." I'm about to ask if she's serious, but I by the look of her face I can see that she is. "He practically told everyone I'm an escort."

"I didn't think you had sex?" I ask carefully.

"We didn't."

"He just made it up?" She nods her head, and she looks embarrassed like *she's* the one who has anything to be ashamed about. I definitely should have let Tramp eat him.

"I've been offered a job in the city. I just can't make it work living here."

"How about your friend's couch?"

"Her boyfriend and his python moved in the moment I was out the door."

"You can't work remote?"

"One day a week, maybe two."

"Why not more?"

"Too many presentations."

"What about online?"

"I don't sell very well online." I don't understand, because Ginny is a stunning woman, she's animated and when she smiles, she lights up the entire room.

"How the hell is that even possible?"

"When I do presentations in real life my enthusiasm shines through, I get exited…" She says something else I don't hear, because the second she says *exited* my mind goes straight to the gutter and I barely repress a groan. "I walk around, I draw on whiteboards, I use my hands…" *use her hands*—please God, yes. My mind makes up all kind of scenarios where she's using her hands.

"Hmm," I say and hope it's not too misplaced. She rambles on about something I don't hear.

"I'm just so pissed at myself. I can't believe I fell for that bullshit."

"Yeah," I mumble and absently nod. I have no idea what she's talking about, but fortunately she's so angry it doesn't seem to matter I have a blank stare on my face.

"I'm thirty, for heaven's sake!" she yells furiously. She turns to me, and I pinch my lips together. "What are you doing?" She asks with a frown.

"I'm not saying anything right now. Pretty sure anything will get me castrated." Ginny snorts.

"Yeah, and we can't have that now you have a dog-sitter, can we?" I shake my head tentatively in agreement.

Great Expectations

Fun fact: Dogs can get separation anxiety—so can people.

It's barely December and people are already starting to get Christmas crazy. They actually started at least a month ago—probably two—because consumers apparently can't live without the stress of one holiday or another. The orange of Halloween has blended seamlessly into the red of Christmas, and none of us know how it happened. I'm already choking on it.

Ginny is at my apartment for her first dog-sitting, so I can meet up with Matt and Hugh, Jeff and Pete at a local bar. The cockblocker is entertained and it's time to catch a glimpse of my old life. The era before Tramp. Scruff is in place, blue T-shirt—to emphasize my eyes—is practically painted on, and jeans. No Christmas sweater—ugly or not—for me, because you can't redeem yourself wearing one of those. Believe me.

"There he is," Matt exclaims loudly as soon as I make it through the door of the bar. God, I've missed this. Women smile at me, they're beautiful, dressed for a night of naughty fun. Lots of legs, cleavage, sexy stilettos. Hands run casually and teasingly over my ass as I make my way to the bar. Hello heaven, my name is Simon—did you miss me?

The only disappointing thing is that none of them—beautiful as they may be—stirs my interest like Ginny does. Compared to Ginny, they are all…lacking somehow. And the strange, happy feeling in my gut whenever I think of her is absent. I decide I don't need that happy feeling—I just need a woman. I've lived my entire life without that feeling, it might be a bonus, but it's not essential for my survival.

I've only just paid for my beer when I feel a hand on my shoulder. I glance down and see long, red nails and that's a splendid way to start the evening. I gladly turn and come face to face with a blonde woman wearing a very short red dress with white, fluffy edges. She looks like Santa's naughty wife and please, call me Saint Nicholas tonight.

"Jillan," she purrs.

"Simon," I say and hold out my hand which she takes.

"I've heard of you."

"Is that a good thing?" She glances down at my groin and bites her lip as she looks at my face again.

"It definitely is."

Do you know that old tv-series 'Baywatch?' It started in 1989, ran for eleven seasons over thirteen years. Two hundred and forty-two episodes, I shite you not. The most famous stars were David Hasselhoff (two hundred and twenty episodes) and Pamela Anderson (hundred and ten episodes). Then there's the movie from 2017 starring The Rock (he'll never be Dwayne to me) and Zack Efron, but I *don't* want to think about that one. Shudder.

Jillian is a hot blond, and she could give Pammy-girl a run for her double D money that's for sure. She bats her eyelashes and tells me her nickname is Jilly or Jilly-girl. She asks if I want to use either one when I fuck her. In return she'll call me daddy if I want to. I don't want to. Not the daddy part at least. Not the nicknames either. I just want to fuck.

We leave only fifteen minutes after I walked into the bar. Destination: Jillian's apartment. Matt groans in jealousy, Jeff rolls his eyes, Pete looks baffled, and Hugh laughs like it's the funniest shite he's ever seen. I have a feeling he'll be collecting money from a bet as soon as I'm out the door.

Another fifteen minutes, and we're naked and in Jillian's bedroom. On the way here, we kissed and groped each other while trying to walk at the same time. I ought to be exited enough to burst, but strangely it takes me a while to get hard— I hadn't expected that. My cock feels like it's been on hunger strike for ages, so why the hell doesn't it gorge itself now pussy is finally on the table?

"Such restraint, Simon," she teases. Like I'm doing it on bloody purpose! "Do you want me to work *hard* for it?" She's on her knees in front of me, looking up at me with huge blue eyes.

"Of course, I do," I say with a smirk.

"Oh, I like that." She pushes me and I let myself fall onto the bed, landing on my back. At my second bounce in the mattress, she already has my cock in her mouth and is sucking it eagerly. God, that feels good. I groan and close my eyes so I can really enjoy it. I need more blowjobs. Once a day—at least—would be nice. My mind starts imagining how it looks with her pale, pink lips sucking me. I groan loudly because that looks so good. Wait a minute…Jillan was wearing red lipstick. I flinch slightly and open my eyes, because thinking of another woman right now is an insanely bad idea. I look at her blond head bobbing up and down as she sucks my cock and that's a pretty good view too.

"So good," I groan, and my hips starts to rock gently because I want this. I want it so much. She looks up at me, smiles, and licks her lips *thoroughly*. A bit too porn movie for my taste, but right now I'll take it.

"Ready for your rodeo?" She asks, and I experience a moment of true fear because I imagine boots with spores, and a riding crop, and I won't be able to stand another animalistic experience. Lindsey, the Cat was plenty. Jillian smiles coyly at my expression, which I'm sure must be a look of horror. "You are hung like a horse and I'm going to ride you like a derby winner," she giggles. Rodeo, derby, whatever—I need a condom before she starts talking about My Little Pony and I lose all enthusiasm. Or The Black Stallion and then I'm going to crack up laughing or make a joke about her being colourblind. Or…ugh…the opportunities for horse analogies are endless.

I grab my jeans on the floor, roam the pockets, and in record time I'm suited up and ready for my ride. I'm *so* ready. Jillian grabs my cock and runs it along her wet pussy and that feels amazing. I flex my hips and silently beg her to let me in, and she does. She cautiously slides down my cock and I clench my teeth. I need to let her take her time, because I *need* her to fuck me—desperately. Her eyes widen slightly when she's taken all of me and I send her a satisfied and grateful smile when she slowly starts rocking her hips. We're not winning a derby like this, that's for sure. But slow and steady wins the race, right? Except that was a tortoise.

Fortunately, Jillian's aware of that too and her movements become faster, more frantic, and I squeeze her ass and push deeper into her. So hot, so soft, so good.

"God, Gin, like that," I groan. The woman who was riding my cock enthusiastically until a second ago freezes.

"What did you call me?"

"Jill," I lie with conviction.

"You know my nickname is Jilly," she pouts.

"Sorry, heat of passion and all…" Thankfully, she accepts the lamest excuse ever. She smiles at me and wiggle a bit on my cock, teasing me. I grab her tits and ease my thumbs over her puckered nipples. "So sexy," I say hoarsely. "And you wonder why I'm losing my mind?" Definitely the right thing to say because she leans into my touch and with a dirty smile, she eagerly starts riding me again. God, I've missed pussy. I haven't spoiled myself like this in ages and I love it.

"Suck me," she pants. I sit up, so I can suck her tits—it's the least I can do because she's doing a really good job. My balls are tightening as she bounces on my cock. She grabs my shoulders and her nails bore into my skin as she fucks me even harder.

"Fuck, that's it, Gin, you feel so good," I say and the second the words are out of my mouth I wince. She stills immediately.

"Simon, what the hell…" I was just about to come, and I want to say something to make her keep going, but let's face it…I got nothing.

"I'm sorry," I sigh, when she scrambles of me.

"You're an asshole," she snarls.

"Yeah, I know." I groan as I rub my face. I really am an asshole.

"Get the hell out of here." I don't say anything. She slams the front door so hard behind me the entire building rattles. I can't really say I blame her, but at least I had time to put my clothes back on.

It's only ten o'clock, I have time. Sex is all about expectations, right?

I enter the first bar I come upon and by some miracle, I see Lucy right away. She's a beautiful woman, she really is. She's sexy as hell and kinky in bed. She's a man-eater and she's after the sex, nothing else. She bites and scratches and likes to be fucked hard with a big cock. You just got to love a woman like that.

She sees me and waves and I hug her fiercely as soon as I've made my way to her.

"What's with you?" She asks curiously once I've let her go.

"I need to fuck a woman who doesn't get pissed if I call her by another name, who'll forgive me for only lasting three minutes because it's been so long. In return I'll go down on her for hours."

"You're pathetic, Simon," she groans.

"I know."

"Where's your monster?"

"If you're talking about my cock, it's in my pants. If you're talking about my dog, it has a sitter tonight."

"What are you saying?"

"Who are you talking about? My cock or my dog?"

"Your dog."

"That's disappointing. My dog-sitter is in town tonight."

"You have a dog-sitter?"

"Yes."

"What took you so long?"

"Waiting for the right…" I bite my tongue before I say woman. "One," I finish.

"Will it be worth my while?"

"You know me."

"I used to. Is it still true?"

"Well of course," I say with a casual shrug like I actually know.

"So, it's been a long time?"

"It has."

"You were a really great fuck back then."

"I haven't lost it if that's what you're worried about." I hope I haven't lost it.

I've lost it. I can't get hard, and I want to kill myself. Two hours after I entered Lucy's apartment, I leave.

"You can't tell anyone about this, okay? It could ruin my whole reputation."

"Then I would be lying," she smirked. I then made her come with my mouth and fingers, and BOB. That's not quite as adventurous as it might seem, because BOB's not a man, it's pink and runs on batteries. I made her promise she wouldn't start a rumour about me being *impotent*—amazing what you can make a woman promise with the help of orgasms. But I didn't enjoy it, not really. So, I'm a great fuck now by reputation only. Apparently, a fake reputation is all a man has.

When I leave Lucy's apartment, I stumble into the first bar I see. It's small and old, not popular, and it's exactly what I need. That and alcohol. I order a triple *gin* and tonic. Ginny drinks *gin* and tonic. I down the drink and order another. And a beer. And another beer.

*

I feel like shite. My head is pounding, and my entire body is sore. Somehow, I've aged from twenty-seven to over a hundred in one night. I might also have gotten lost, because I have absolutely no idea where I am. I hear large paws shuffling across the floor and they stop just beside me. I don't have to open my eyes to know I at least made it home. And I'm on the floor for some reason.

"Go away," I groan without opening my eyes. Something smells funny.

Whine.

"I mean it."

Panting.

"Fuck off."

Paws tapping.

"Pretend I'm not home."

Whimper.

"Leave me alone."

Whine.

"Talk to your sitter."

Loud bark!

My entire body twitches and I reluctantly open one eye—and then I jerk away, startled. Tramp is standing right beside me, and he had his snout about two inches from my nose. At least that explains the funny smell and thank God, it's too early for canned dog food.

"Jesus, Tramp," I say and put a hand over my chest, like that can somehow slow my frantically beating heart.

Wagging.

"Are you trying to kill me?"

Blank stare and cocked head.

"I think you're able to do that yourself." I look up and see Ginny coming into the living room. She hands me a glass of water and two pills as I slowly sit up.

"Why am I hugging my door mat?" I ask. Because I am indeed holding on to my door mat like it's a lifeline. Ginny shrugs and I gratefully accept the pills and water.

"I found you sleeping in the hallway right in front of the door. You'd pulled the door mat over you."

"Really?"

"Yeah," Ginny says looking resigned. "You wouldn't let go of it."

"How long was I out there?" I can't help thinking about Samuel and my heart starts pounding again.

"About five minutes, I think. Tramp alerted me."

"Why am I not in bed?"

"You refused. I'm a dog-sitter, not a babysitter for a grown man acting like a toddler."

"We always act like toddlers," I say defensively and hug my door mat like I'm Linus Van Pelt and it's my security blanket.

There Is No Heaven—Probably Not for Dogs Either

Fun fact: The Bible doesn't say anything about dogs going to heaven. It says you should beware of them—Tramp has proven that countless times. "For without [are] dogs, and sorcerers, and whoremongers, and murderers, and idolaters, and whosoever loveth and maketh a lie."

Friday the next week, I tell myself the reason I couldn't get properly laid was because I knew Ginny was at my apartment, and that's the reason I was thinking about her that much. That's all. I'm getting desperate and I'm not certain desperation is going to help my…I don't even want to think about it. The thought makes me panicky and sweaty. Stress can cause *the I-word*. Maybe this is Tramp's fault too?

I got off work at four am, and it took me almost five hours to drive back and forth to Ginny's place. Told you, I'm desperate. At least I'm not depended on several trains like Ginny is. When I left Tramp with Ginny, he was so thrilled to see her, he didn't give a shite I was leaving. They grow up so fast.

At home in my apartment, I look around and I listen. The apartment is quiet. Quiet is good right? Except it's making me jittery. But I'm really going to appreciate it later tonight when

I bring a woman here. There'll be no barking, no whimpering, no cockblocking of any kind. It's going to be great. Right? The place is awfully quiet. It doesn't quite feel like home. It feels empty and I look around to see if anything's missing. I don't think I've been robbed, but it still feels strange. I glance at the phone. I open a window. I need fresh air. I shower. I wonder around the place and I'm a bit bored. I make coffee and sit down. I get up and look out the window. It's dark so there's not much to see besides the light from the lamp posts four storeys down. I glance at the phone. I order pizza, but it feels wrong. There's no one here to bark at the delivery boy— and scare him to death. There's no one her to eat the crusts and it feels strange tossing them in the bin. I even consider saving them for when Tramp gets home. I finally pick up the phone and call Ginny.

"Do you miss him already?" She asks laughing as a way of greeting. I'm *not* answering that.

"How's he doing?"

"Sleeping like the dead. We went for a walk."

"Did he give you any trouble?"

"Not at all. We even said hello to some goats, and nobody got eaten."

"Impressive."

"One of the goats nipped his tail though." I laugh at this and talk to Ginny a few minutes. She assures me everything is going to be fine, and I need not worry about anything besides getting laid.

I stare at the phone when I hang up. I'm smiling like an idiot. I look around the apartment. I'm a bit bored. I go to bedroom and put on clothes for a night out. Matt texts me, asks me where I am. I suppose I should be going. My phone dings and I quickly unlock it to see the message. Ginny has sent a photo of Tramp and the goats. One of the goats looks like it's in the middle of a very loud baa and Tramp has his head pulled back like he's surprised by the sound. It's hilarious and I laugh out loud. It feels so strange. And no one is there to look curiously at me. I'd better get going. I'm meeting my friends at the bar and heaven…here I come.

At eleven thirty, I'm back in heaven. Women smile at me, they're beautiful, dressed for a night of naughty fun. Lots of legs, cleavage, sexy stilettos. Hands run casually and teasingly over my ass as I make my way to the bar and…I feel claustrophobic. I go to the bar and order a beer—no more *gin* and tonics for me that's for sure.

I'm feeling frazzled when I get to the table where my friends are at. Pretty sure I'm sweating too.

"What's wrong with you?" Hugh asks.

"Are women always that handsy? It's annoying as hell." I sit down and my friends look at me, concern clear on their faces.

"Do you need a hospital?" Matt asks seriously and lays a hand on my shoulder. He's got a frown on his face, and he suddenly looks remarkably sober for someone who's been drinking for hours.

"I don't think they will take him," Jeff says and shakes his head.

"Didn't you date a nurse?" Hugh asks Matt.

"No, just fucked her. Besides, we need a psychologist for him."

"I'm sitting right here, you know?" I say irritably. This is *not* my night—either.

"We know," Hugh says and pats my hand gently like I need to be reassured of my own existence. I don't. I don't think so at least. Pete stands up abruptly and leaves the table and Hugh glances my way like he's expecting me to have an anxiety attack because of the sudden movement.

"You, my friend, are about to be cured," Matt says with a dirty grin. I look at him, and then I look at Pete who's returned to the table with a woman. I don't really see her. I see long legs, short skirt, pale skin, dark boots. She's in my lap within moments, talking to me. She's beautiful—she really is—but she irritates me. She's probably another cephalopod. I don't know her name, but I'm certain she's told me—I just didn't listen.

I'm in my car at one o'clock. I pull up in front of Ginny's house at two-thirty. Tramp's barking but it sounds more enthusiastic than threatening. Ginny opens the door and Tramp comes rushing out to greet me. I absently pat his head and look at Ginny. Her hair is a mess, she's wearing a green, silk pyjamas, and she looks like the most amazing thing I've ever seen in my life.

"Simon, what the hell…" She doesn't get to finish her question before I kiss her. I press my body against hers and the feel of their tits is making me groan in appreciation. Her tongue slides into my mouth and that's when I know she truly is an angel—a horny one that is. I'm as hard as I've ever been as we stumble up the stairs. I haven't lost shite—I just needed the right woman.

In her bedroom, I kiss her jaw and her neck slowly. I linger with my mouth over her skin so I can lick and suck it and taste it. She moans slightly as I start to unbutton her pyjamas top. I'm desperate, but I want to savour every second despite the anticipation might actually kill me. Someone with a doctorate will tell I'm exaggerating and it's not possible, but I'm convinced it is.

Finally—fucking finally—I get to touch her gorgeous tits. I gently cup them as I suck and lick and take in every part of her. Her skin smells delicious, her breathing is soft and moaning, and it's making me euphoric.

I slide my hand lower and lower and…I can feel the heat from her pussy when I run my fingers through her curls, and she adjusts her stance slightly to give me room to get my fingers where we both want them. I groan against her skin when I reach my destination. She's sobbing wet and…perfect. I pull the pyjama bottoms down and they pool on the floor at her feet as I tease and tempt and gives her all the attention I've been wanting to do for months.

"I need you," she moans and staggers backwards to the bed.

She lies down naked on the bed, legs slightly bent and spread, like an offering for me and I take in every part of her. I feel her eyes roam my body as well as I quickly strip in front of her. I want her to see all of me and I love the way her eyes widen slightly when she looks at my cock. That never gets old, but this time it's better than it's ever been before. This time it matters.

Without a word, I crawl on the bed and settle between her legs. My cock is practically reaching for her with the first drops of pre-cum, and I can't wait to feel her.

"I'm not on the pill," she whimpers. She's not on the pill, I don't have a condom, but I'm not stopping anything.

"I'm clean and besides that I don't give a shite, we'll make another baby."

"You've got a baby?" She asks confused.

"A furry one," I say with a grin and slowly push into her. I'm enraptured and I watch closely as she takes every inch of me. Shivers run down my spine at the sight of it.

"Shit, Simon, you're huge."

"And you're so fucking tight," I moan. God, she feels good. So warm, so soft, so tight—amazing. Her pussy is hugging my cock like it's saying: 'welcome home' and this is exactly what it feels like. Home. I'm such a cheesy bastard. But at least I'm finally having sex—and with the woman I apparently want more than anyone. I was truly deluded when I thought heaven was at a bar with beautiful, touchy women. I was a complete moron, because this…this is my heaven.

*

Remember when I told you that lack of sex will turn a grown and *extremely* capable man into a teenager if he's not careful. Unfortunately, that is very true. Fifteen minutes later, I roll off Ginny. I didn't last nearly, as long, as I'd hoped—but definitely longer than I thought. And feared.

"I'll make it up to you, I swear," I say and kiss her as I pull her close.

"I'm happy," she says casually.

"I know. I heard." I grin and my stomach clenches at the mere thought of Ginny's throaty voice demanding 'give me.' I'm still out of breath and I still don't feel like I've had enough. When you're twenty-seven, unfortunately, you might come as fast as a teenager, but equally unfortunate: the refractory period doesn't correspond. That is *so* disappointing. But it feels good lying like this with Ginny. It's about three in the morning, I'm so tired, but my mind and my body won't let me sleep.

"You sounded pretty happy too," she giggles, and she's right. I might have exalted her pussy, it's basically a divinity by now. And I'm a very religious man. Or animal rather, because the sounds I was making was barely human.

"On your stomach," I demand. "I want to do something I've thought about for ages."

"What's that?"

"Lick your tattoo." She giggles as she slowly turns. The tattoo is on her lover back and I'm going to enjoy making my way there. Only when she turns completely, I see it's not a tramp stamp—it's a delicate corset and lace tattoo. What I thought was a tramp stamp is where the lace and corset ends, and it looks like it's been casually left open. It starts at the middle of her back.

"Jesus Christ," I croak. I've never seen anything so sexy in my entire life. She laughs softly but it turns into loud moaning when I lick her spine. My nerves twitch, but there's no sound from the living room downstairs.

I kiss every single brush stroke of her tattoo. Her skin is soft and warm, and I rub my stubbled cheek against it. Feather-light touches with my fingers drive her wild and I must say I can't recall a single instance, where foreplay and a woman's pleasure has mattered so much. I move my fingers between her legs, and she gets up on all fours like she too can't wait any longer.

"You're lifting tail for me?" I ask. I'm already panting in anticipation.

"Just like the vet," she says with a smirk, and I moan torturedly.

"Never should have told you that story."

"It was funny."

"For you perhaps," I line up my cock and I push hard into her from behind, wanting to punish her for teasing me. "Shite, Ginny," I moan. I'm losing my mind. Her pussy is so hot, so soft, so wet, and ready for me. I rub my chest against her back as I start to fuck her slowly. Jesus, she feels good.

"I'm going to come," she moans.

"Let me feel you." I want her to milk me, I want her pussy to suck all of my come into her. And I want to do this forever.

"Simon," she's panting desperately in a whining voice. She sounds like she's in pain, I know she's not, because I feel the same way. I feel her pussy clench, it's like a powerful silky glove. One that will hopefully never let me go.

*

When I wake up, I have absolutely no idea what time it is. Ginny's sleeping and I carefully get out of bed not to disturb her. I make my way downstairs and go into the hallway where Ginny has made a bed for Tramp consisting of pillows and blankets. He looks very comfortable, and I truly feel like a crazy dog owner because I got him the ridiculously large and expensive orthopaedic bed at home. Tramp wakes up, then he raises his head and looks at me. Then he groans, wags his tail slightly, and lies back down. I pet his rough fur as I dazedly contemplate that strange, unknown feeling inside me. When Tramp grunts, I take this as a sign for me to sod off, and I gladly do.

I make my way upstairs and creep back into bed with Ginny, who stirs when I lie down. God, I'm so tired.

"How's your baby?" I can tell by the tone of her voice she's smiling. Funny thing to know about a woman.

"You tell me in about a month or so," I say and kiss her shoulder.

"Idiot," she scoffs, but I can still hear her smile.

"There's no pharmacy here, is there?" I ask.

"Yes, but it's not open 24 hours a day."

"Everyone in the village will know it if I buy all the condoms in store tomorrow, won't they?"

"Ten minutes tops."

"And confront me about if whenever I meet anyone?"

"They'd probably require details. Ask me if you were any good."

"Easy question," I say confidently.

"Well, there's a rumour in the city…" I instantly panic and I dread Lucy hasn't kept her promise about me and…the *I-word!*

"Which rumour?"

"About this insanely hot man with a great ass and huge cock. He's supposed to be the most amazing fuck."

"Really?" I ask casually like it isn't *me* she's talking about.

"Yeah, a blond man. Do you know him?"

"What?" I snap and despite I know she was—hopefully—teasing me my masculine ego demands revenge!

I switch on the light and tear the duvet to the side. Ginny pinches her eyes at the sudden brightness in the room. I can see her all of her gorgeous naked body and I settle between her legs.

"You idiot, what are you doing?" she complains loudly.

"I want to look at you, when I do this…" I say as I push my cock into her as deep as I can. She moans and closes her eyes again. I don't look at her face, my gaze is fixed where I piston in and out of her slick heat. I'm certain I'm on the brink of sensory overload, Ginny will get all the bragging rights about this night if I faint. And right now, I just don't care.

"You're insatiable," she moans. She's definitely done complaining.

"Making up for lost time," I pant. "With you."

I stumble down the stairs what I'm certain is only a few hours later. My muscles are sore, and I think I might have sprained something. I'm freezing when I come downstairs, and I wonder if the boiler has shut down during the night. I don't think so, because upstairs was warm enough. I go into hallway to assure Tramp we're going for a walk in a few minutes, and he doesn't need to panic, stomp upstairs, and jump into the bed with us—or whatever he was contemplating. As it turns out, there's no reason to tell him and I know now why it was so cold coming downstairs. The front door is open. Tramp is gone.

Houdini Has Fur

Fun fact: Dog owners are insane. Truly. There's no easy way to say it.

I've lost my dog and my marbles, my patience, my common sense, and I'm nowhere near ordinary dog owner crazy behaviour. I'm way beyond, because my dog is missing. I'm not quite certain for how long, but my money is on since the first light of day when he usually drags me to the park. What I don't understand is how the hell he got out the front door. We didn't lock it last night, but it was definitely closed. This means something or *someone* has opened it.

You read all kinds of horror stories about dog fights. How family dogs are kidnapped and used as easy victims and put up for slaughter in a dog fighting arena. Thinking about it makes me sick. Tramp's too large to be used as a bait dog—I think. But what if they tape his mouth shut? What if they let two or three dogs loose at the same time?

Ginny has activated the locals. The whole bloody village has a Facebook group—and their own local detective. She's not called Miss Marple, but she looks like her—Joan Hickson of course. She, by the way, starred in all twelve episodes of the BBC series and she was also encouraged by Agatha Christie herself to play the part.

The village's detective is Helen Donaghy and contrary to Miss Marple, she wears trousers and boots like she's about to climb Mount Everest. She wears a red military-looking wool jacket—it's probably original vintage—and a light blue beret. Also contrary to Miss Marple, she has the mien of a hardened colonel. And when she slams a card of the village down on Ginny's dining room table and considers strategies, she looks like one too. I'm not ashamed to admit I'm a little intimidated. She studies the map and mumbles something about topography and evasive manoeuvres and easy access to food and water and shelter. I think Napoleon himself might have raised an impressed eyebrow.

The village is so small, the dog is so big—how the hell can he hide like this? But he might be kidnapped, and he might be on an aircraft on his way to Russia or Eastern Europe to be slaughtered at this very moment. They *eat* dogs in China—do they import them too? He might also just have run far away on his own and is having a great time being a free dog at last. And he didn't even have to build a rocket.

The only good thing about this is I'm staying at Ginny's house. And I'm sleeping in her bed. Naked. She's wrapped around me, and did I mention she's naked too? Heaven is *definitely not* at a bar with women all around me—heaven is being with Ginny in bed and seeing her as the first thing in the morning. My first thought: Wow! I could get used to a view like this.

I call work Monday morning and my boss grudgingly gives me a week off. It might have something to do with me shrieking like a teenage girl and blabbering about Eastern Europe and small villages. He made me promise I'd see a doctor.

*

We go on endless walks, calling out Tramp's name to no avail. Thursday afternoon Ginny gets a call from Helen Donaghy. I don't know what she is saying, but I clearly hear her barking out information like a general giving orders.

"We need to see Mrs Fletcher," Ginny says determined when she's hung up the phone. She looks equally amused and exasperated.

"Why?"

"She swears she saw a werewolf in her vegetable garden last night."

"Could be him." But vegetable garden? That sounds highly unlikely—unless he got lost.

I might've sounded unlikely, but when I see Mrs Fletcher's vegetable garden there's no doubt in my mind the werewolf, she saw last night was in fact Tramp. Nobody but him can make a mess like this.

"It ate my carrots, why would a werewolf do that?" She asks confused.

"I don't think it was a werewolf, Mrs Fletcher," Ginny says gently. "It was a dog."

"Poppycock. It was a werewolf."

"Did it look something like this?" I ask and hold out my phone to show her a picture of Tramp. She looks at the screen and then she looks at me in awe.

"It's your werewolf?"

"It is," I say. "I'm so sorry about your garden."

"I thought werewolves were carnivores," she says, looking even more confused.

"He's on a diet," I say drily, and I try to ignore Ginny who looks like she's about to burst with laughter.

"Oh," Mrs Fletcher says. She frowns like she's trying to make sense of it. Good luck with that.

When we leave Mrs Fletcher's ruined garden, I'm at least comforted that Tramp is not on his way to Eastern Europe. Mrs Fletcher wouldn't accept any compensation because she is quite certain she can charge the other villager's admission to see the werewolf's destruction. She was looking for cardboard and markers to draw up a sign when we left.

"You know, you'll be officially named the Wolfman in village, right?" Ginny asks.

"Thought I might," I sigh. But at least, Tramp's not on his way to a dog fighting arena or a Chinese dinner table. Yet. Which means he's still mine to castrate or kill.

And speaking of balls…Every man should manscape, you know? For you fuckers who believe it has something to do with homosexuality or metro sexuality or you mind it for another invalid reason—forget it. This has to do with a man's most developed instinct: selfishness. If you want your balls sucked along with your cock, you make sure they are shaven smooth. That's what I've done, and when we get home from Mrs Fletcher, I get my reward. It might be a pity blowjob because I'm sad—and has gone mad—because Tramp's missing, but that's irrelevant. I still love tea-bagging.

"Suck like that," I groan. "Harder." And she does. Ginny's phone rings, but fortunately, she doesn't answer it. Right now, I don't care if this is *the* phone call that can save Tramp's life—I want this too much.

When she's done with me, I'm certain I must be wearing a very silly smile—I still look terribly masculine of course—

and this truly is heaven. I definitely had the right idea when I wanted a woman to spoil me every day. Ginny looks happy too and that's another way she spoils me. She reaches for her phone and then frowns slightly when she returns the call.

"Hey, Helen." Ginny listens and then sits up abruptly. "We'll be there directly." What is that frown? Why isn't she smiling? Probably because Tramp's an asshole, that's why. But what has happened? Do they have dog fighting on a nearby farm? Or does a local dish include dog meat? Maybe they export it?

"What?" I ask nervously.

"They've found him. Helen has caught him at Chapman's farm."

*

Ginny is driving. She races down the narrow roads faster than I would ever have dared, and I swear the shortcut she suddenly takes is only a path. The four-wheel drive finally comes to good use as Ginny balances the large car on the edge of a ditch in what I would have deemed an impossible act. If I had to guess my Range Rover—which always drives on roads, preferably asphalted—has just had an orgasm when we arrive at Chapman's farm. Helen Donaghy is standing outside the barn. With practiced hand signals she guides Ginny to park the car to exact spot she wants, like Ginny is trying to fit the Range Rover into a tight parking spot. She's not—it's in the middle of the courtyard.

Helen leads us into the barn, and there he is…The bane of my existence is right in front of me. He got caught by an old Miss Marple-looking woman and I wish he was human so I could mock him daily about it. If he was human, I could punch him too. Repeatedly. But if he really was human, he'd be too big and too strong for me to do anything—besides serving as a punching bag. I prefer him as a dog, and besides, I can still mock him for my own pleasure.

They've put him in a horse box, fitting considering he's the size of a pony. Was he this big before he ran away? He probably was, but somehow, I've forgotten. Inside the box he wags his tail and whines delighted—like he does when he welcomes me home every day after work. Doesn't he understand how monumental this is? Doesn't he understand how worried I've been? How stressful these last few days have been? Looking at him, the answer is no. God, I'm disappointed.

"I've already called the vet," Helen informs us. "He'll be here shortly."

Ginny and I go into the horse box, and Tramp is delighted. I bite my cheek because now is not the time to cry—the manly way of course—and I refuse to let Tramp think I've missed him, since he obviously thinks nothing of several days of separation. He truly is an asshole.

"Looks like the vicar's cat got a hold of his ear," Ginny says and carefully lifts his left ear. It's shredded—but it also looks like it's been healing for a few days. It's caked in mud and scab, and he doesn't seem to be in any pain when Ginny carefully rubs it to get some of the dirt of. Pity.

The local vet treats mostly cows and horses. Tramp is almost the size of a calf, and they're keeping him in a horsebox, so that will probably do fine. He arrives only ten minutes after Ginny and I and fortunately Tramp has worked off most of his enthusiasm by now.

"He was shot," the vet declares just as he opens the door to the horse box. He's nowhere near Tramp so unless he has superpowers, he can't know that. Unless he instantly recognises, what an asshole Tramp is and concludes he *should* be shot. I think I might agree.

"How do you know?" Ginny asks.

"Erhm…It might have been my mother," the vet says and coughs into his hand.

"What?" I whine.

"Only birdshot," he ensures me. I look at the vet. He's got grey hair and wrinkles, like an elephant's ass and there's no way he's under seventy. Makes you wonder how old his mother is—and how the hell she's still wielding a riffle.

The vet shaves Tramp's bum and I've got to say I'm a vindictive bastard because this pleases me beyond. He then jams in a syringe with sedation with the same finesse as when using a captive-bolt pistol. Tramp flinches, but Ginny soothes him, and the vet is able to remove the birdshots. Sterile drapes are apparently overrated. When he's done—I have no idea if he got all of the birdshots out—he slams two zipper bags in my hand with no label on them. This looks very much like a drug deal.

"For the pain. And in case of infection," the vet says.

"Are those for animals?" Ginny asks suspiciously.

"Why shouldn't they be?" he says and shrugs.

Because I'm curious I shove Tramp onto the scale they have in the barn. It's normally used for cows, horses, goats, sheep, pigs—and now dogs. We all look at the scale and then we look at each other.

"Does that thing work properly?" Ginny asks, looking stunned, and the vet nods silently. I've got a *hundred and seventy*-pound dog standing on the scale, wagging his tail happily. I hope to God he's done growing.

*

Tramp's running away was apparently the most exciting thing to happen in the village for quite some time. Helen posed for a photo with Tramp, she posed for a photo with Tramp and the vet, she posed for a photo with me and Tramp, she posed for several photos alone, she posed for a photo with me and Tramp and Ginny—and they were all posted in the village's Facebook group. Ginny was described as the beautiful, local woman who offered shelter to the 'Wolfman,' the owner of the werewolf creature loose in the area. Mrs Fletcher's vegetable garden was even mentioned and I'm certain she's delighted, and I'm certain her business has picked up. I was described as the *handsome*, but helpless, city *boy* and now I'm even more happy about my decision about *not* buying condoms here. I have a feeling whatever absurd scenario I could come up with, would be an understatement compared to reality.

Friday morning, I'm sitting at the steps to the garden. Ginny is making breakfast and I've only just come home from my morning walk with Tramp, who acts like nothing out of the ordinary has happened this week. He is such an asshole. Tramp looks me like he doesn't understand why I'm sitting here. He probably doesn't, and I don't quite know either.

"Are you mad at me?" I ask.

Wagging tail.

"Not even because I had sex with Ginny?"

Wagging tail.

"I really like her."

Happy bark and wagging tail.

"You think she fancies me too?"

Whimper.

"Not at all?"

Frown.

"I'm going to ask her. I want to go out with her."

Whimper.

"You're horrible for a man's ego, you know?"

Smirk.

"You really don't like me?" I ask sadly.

Whimper and he lays down on his back.

"You want another human?"

Gets up and howls like an insane Husky. Probably a drugged, insane Husky since I've fed him a few of the pills the vet gave me. I still have no idea what kind of pills they are.

Ginny comes into the garden, but Tramp continues his concert, and I don't even ask him to shut up despite he's right in front of me and making a Godawful noise that might make me deaf. I'm perfectly fine letting him suffer even if he's making a racket.

"What's going on?" Ginny asks, looking confused at Tramp's howling.

"I asked him if he wanted another human." Tramp has now made it to the death of the harmonica in his rather extensive repertoire and Ginny's struggling to keep a straight face, which I appreciate. I'm not sure Tramp will forgive either of us if we start laughing at his immense suffering. He scrambles to his feet and pushes his enormous head between my arms and lays it on my leg. He's whimpering and wagging his tail.

"Simon, stop teasing," Ginny snaps.

"You're lucky to have her," I tell Tramp and finally pet him. He leans into me with a grumbling sound in his chest and it almost sounds like he's purring. I'm not ruling out cat in this mixed-breed yet that's for sure.

The Good, the Bad and the Ugly

Fun fact: In dogs' sexual and reproductive habits, female dogs are referred to as 'bitches.' In slang, bitches is a vulgar expression for a female. Male dogs on the other hand are referred to as 'studs.' In slang, it means a man who is notably virile and sexually active.

I reluctantly drive home Saturday. I spend a lot of time kissing Ginny goodbye and I truly don't want to leave. Only five miles from her house, Tramp starts whimpering and not even putting on his favourite playlist makes him happy. Stopping at the roadside earns me the same look of confusion as it did the last time. We stop at McDonald's even if I rarely feed him anything but dog food. The Quarter Pounder disappears in his mouth and he only chews three times before swallowing the entire thing. I was so naive thinking he might enjoy it just twenty seconds.

Matt, Pete, Hugh, and Jeff are coming over for poker tonight. I'm looking forward to it, but my thoughts stray to Ginny. I want to call her and it's ridiculous, because I just saw her this morning. Tramp shuffles about in the apartment like he too has to get used to being home. The day passes slowly, and I'm relieved when there's a knock on the door and my friends barge into the apartment like they live here.

Within minutes, we are all seated at the table. Pete is shuffling the cards, and Jeff is opening beers. We are going to be hung-over tomorrow for sure. I almost look forward to the numbness.

"Why did you shave Tramp?" Hugh asks when he sees the shaved spots on Tramp's bum.

"The vet did. He was shot."

"Why did you shoot him?" Jeff asks.

"*I* didn't." My friends glance at each other like they don't quite believe me. I don't blame them because I'd be lying if I said the thought hadn't crossed my mind.

"Where's the bloody gin?" Matt shouts, and I cringe. Please don't…I hear the sound of enthusiastic paws stomping through the apartment, and Tramp enters the living room. He's wagging his tail and eyeing everything like he's looking for something.

"What's with him?" Jeff asks.

"Matt just said the name of his favourite human."

"No, I didn't. I asked for *gin*," Matt says and I groan loudly. Tramp dashes to him and looks at him expectantly.

"I thought you were his favourite human?" I shake my head.

"Not even close."

"Ouch."

"It's a two-hour drive," I say with a smirk towards Matt. Tramp is staring him down at the moment and Matt is squirming in the chair like he's about to be waterboarded. Dogs can do that to you.

I don't want to think about the two-hour drive, I don't want to think about Ginny, but as always, I can't help myself. And then there's that unknown feeling. I fold my arms on the table and lay my chin on them.

"What's with you?" Hugh asks.

"Tramp ran away when we were at Ginny's." Tramp starts tapdancing in front of Matt and I send him to his ridiculously large and expensive orthopaedic bed. He scowls but by now he has probably learned we're all just torturing him, talking about Ginny. I'll be the only one paying the price for this later of course.

"Did you get him back?" Matt asks. I nod and roll my eyes. "Obviously."

"Sorry about that?" Matt asks, looking confused.

"No."

"So, what is it?"

"I fucked Ginny." So many times, it'll actually be a miracle if she doesn't get pregnant.

"Finally," Hugh groans.

"Was it a bad fuck or something?" Jeff asks disbelievingly.

"No."

"Then what the hell is wrong with you?" Pete wants to know.

"I think I'm in love with her." The silence around the table is almost eerie. My friends glance at each other and put their heads together. They whisper like it does any good, which it doesn't, considering I'm sitting right beside them.

"Do you think he suffered some kind of shock when Tramp ran away?"

"Should we take him to the hospital?"

"One of us should fuck a psychologist regularly, so we have one close by."

"Maybe we should take turns watching him."

"Should we hire a nurse or a caretaker or something?"

"I should probably be the one fucking the psychologist."

"Do you think it's contagious?" Matt looks truly horrified.

*

I talk to Ginny on the phone every day. We even video chat and Tramp participates happily—but very confused. He doesn't quite understand he can hear Ginny's voice, but not see her or smell her. I feel very superior.

Needless to say, he's delirious with happiness when Ginny comes by the apartment Friday night. She's been desperately looking for the smallest and cheapest office space she can find in the entire city. One where there's a lock on the door, where the toilet is not a bucket in the corner, and where the draught doesn't feel like a hurricane. So far, she has been unsuccessful.

When she enters, I take her coat and then I kiss her. Thoroughly. I've missed her and to myself I can admit I don't like being away from her. That's probably a side effects when you fall in love with someone.

"Ginny, I've been thinking," I say when I can finally bring myself to let go of her.

"And now you want me to take you to the emergency room because of the pain?"

"You are so funny."

"I know," she says and wiggles her eyebrows.

"How would you feel about having a place to stay during the week in the city?"

"What do you mean?"

"And come home on weekends. Like you used to."

"That would be ideal."

"Even if it comes with a man and his dog?"

"What are you saying?"

"Move in with me during the week, and I move in with you in weekends."

"Is this your way of asking me if I want to date you?"

"It is," I say seriously, because this feels very important. "I really like you, Ginny." Understatement.

"I know."

"The not platonic kind of like."

"I know that too."

"Really? How?" Besides the fact I must have fucked her a hundred times by now and still haven't had enough.

"Remember the time you got really drunk and woke up on the floor?"

"What has that got to do with anything?"

"You were plastered when you got home, and you looked at me and told me I was really pretty, but there was another woman you couldn't stop thinking about and you wanted her to be your girlfriend."

"Really?" I have no recollection whatsoever about this, and that is very disturbing.

I have a rule for myself: if I'm too drunk to roll on the condom in one single fluent motion then I'm too drunk to fuck. I have a feeling my drinking might require another rule.

"You told me you probably couldn't get hard without thinking about her anyway."

"Wow," I say drily because that is really disconcerting. I have no idea where this is going, and I think I might kill myself if she tells me I spent the night crying with my head in her lap because I couldn't get laid.

"You told me her name was Ginny." Phew.

"Never thought I'd say it, but apparently drunk me is smarter than sober me."

"It would appear so."

"It's true, though," I say gently. Falling in love is new to me, and I need to get used to it. *And* make sure it's not just a stomach ache, before I tell her.

"You say the sweetest things," she says grinning. She lays her hands on my neck and pull me down so she can kiss me. She can laugh at me all she likes as long as she kisses me too. It only takes moments for my cock to demonstrate I was in fact telling the truth when I told her I needed her to get hard.

"I need to show you my bedroom," I moan as I kiss her and thank God, she follows me eagerly.

I finally have Ginny in my bedroom, and do you know what she asks as soon as she enters? It's not what I was hoping for, I'll tell you that.

"Why do you have a poster of The Good, the Bad and the Ugly in your bedroom?"

"Why not?" Truth is, that poster can hang everywhere and look good. It's iconic.

"Is the ugly anal or something?" She asks.

"I don't like anal."

"I know. That's why I'm asking."

"You can be good, I can be bad, and Tramp's the ugly one."

"Don't call him that," Ginny says and smacks my arm. She looks speculatively at the poster and that doesn't bode well, does it?

"I prefer Lady and the Tramp. Let's get a new poster."

"What about me then?" I ask even if I'm not taking down The Good, the Bad and the Ugly poster. No way. It's an original re-release poster—you know from the time where movie bragging was about Technicolor and Techni scope and not 3D or 4K or something like that.

"You can live here too," she allows.

Do you know that old Walt Disney animated film 'Lady and the Tramp' from 1955? It's an adaptation based on the 1945 Cosmopolitan magazine story 'Happy Dan, The Cynical Dog' by Ward Greene. And it's the 15th Disney animated feature film. It was COLOR BY Technicolor and the first all-cartoon feature in cinema scope. And please, for the love of God—and my sanity—please don't make me talk about the sequel from 2001 and the ones for the streaming service. The 1955 poster now hangs right beside The Good, the Bad and the Ugly. Honestly, it looks kind of strange, but Ginny's happy, and posters don't play theme songs, so Tramp is happy too. I'm happy, because most nights, when I go to bed, Ginny's there. And she's there in the morning when I wake up too. I truly love the view.

*

Ginny's freelance work has finally picked up, and she's busy. Very busy. As it turned out, Ginny isn't the only one her former boss tried to exploit one way or another. He now has a lawsuit—and probably a castration—coming up any time soon.

Do you know the movie 'What Women Want' from 2000? It's starring Mel Gibson—I can't believe it's the same man who made Braveheart five years prior—and Helen Hunt. Gibson plays a cocky, chauvinistic advertising executive who thinks everything can be solved with an advertisement with a bikini babe. He has an accident and magically acquires the ability to hear what women are thinking. He realises that most women, especially at work, and including his psychologist, dislike him and consider him sleazy.

The more Ginny tells me about her boss, I get more and more convinced he's just like Gibson's character—except Ginny's boss doesn't have the epiphany to save him. The agency Ginny worked at has apologised to her and attempted to get her back, but she has declined. They wouldn't listen to anything she had to say when they fired her and now, they're paying for it. Ginny has gotten *a lot* of female clients—many of them former clients at the agency where she worked. Long overdue I think *they* have finally had that epiphany.

Her laptop is running like a Mercedes, fast and smooth and constantly. If I wasn't so attractive, I don't think I'd be able to pull her away from it. She's always working, desperate to increase her savings. The house, she's so reluctant to part with, has been in the family for about two hundred years. It's not opulent or worth much, but it holds the story of generations of her family—it's like a tribute to the common man.

She persuades me to let Tramp celebrate Christmas at her house—amazing what you can make a man promise with the help of orgasms. I make about a hundred disclaimers about the destruction of the Christmas tree, ornaments, socks, and all the things I haven't considered.

Whereas most people take time off between Christmas and the New Year, my boss thinks we should all work, because everyone else is taking time off. Usually, it doesn't bother me and I always volunteer, but this year it bothers me. My parents insist I spend Christmas with them, so I won't see Ginny—and Tramp—for about a week. I also have to meet up with my friends to celebrate Hugh's birthday. This, of course, means we're going out.

'Heaven' has turned into a special kind of hell to me. I used to appreciate women touching me. Now…I can't tell you how much I hate it. I still dance, but nowhere near as close as I used to. When women touch me, or grab me, I quickly peel their hands of me and I can't believe I once wanted cephalopods. There's one sitting beside me right now and I think she might have left an imprint on my ass of her suctions cups despite I'm wearing jeans.

"Are you taking me home, Simon?" She asks and batters her eyelids no doubt in an attempt to flirt.

"No," I say casually. Pete groans torturedly from the other side of the table like I've just made a huge mistake. I haven't.

"What do you mean no?"

"No means no, right?" Objectively speaking, Natalie is *by far*, the most attractive women in the bar and she could easily pass for a runway model. Long legs, slender body, perky tits, and a wide mouth that can easily take two cocks at the same time. Fantastic visual but that's not what I dream about.

"But why not?" She looks genuinely perplexed and I'm certain she's rarely told no.

"Going home to my girl."

"I thought your dog was a boy." Matt guffaws at this and it proves how much Tramp has taken over my life. By now, nobody seems to think anything of it.

"He is."

"Why not then?" She asks, confusion clear on her face.

"I've got the most amazing woman waiting for me at home."

"You have?" She still looks puzzled, like it's an improbability a woman would ever wait for me.

"*I* haven't," Pete interjects and almost throws himself over the table in order to get her attention.

Ginny is not exactly waiting for me at home, but that's none of Natalie's business. Ginny is spending Christmas with her parents at her house. Tramp is with her and that gives me all the freedom in the world to.

A: Do whatever I want with whoever I want. B: Regret I told her I wanted to date her. C: Miss her like crazy. D: Miss Tramp too. I'm going for C. And maybe D—not that I'll ever admit it.

Apparently, Miracles Happen

Fun fact: The word tangled (/'taŋgld/) is an adjective. Among other thing it means: complicated and confused; chaotic.

Do you know the movie 'Invasion of the Body Snatchers' from 1978? It starred Donald Sutherland, Brooke Adams, Jeff Goldblum, and Veronica Cartwright among others. It was based on Jack Finney's novel and it's the second of several adaptations. I've never forgotten that last scene of the movie. Unknowingly to the audience, Donald Sutherland has been body snatched and he betrays Veronica Cartwright, who so far has managed to keep herself alive among the body snatchers, with a horrifying pig-like shriek.

That's pretty much my life now because my friends think I've been overtaken by aliens. I don't get plastered on New Year's Eve because I know I need to be able to drive tomorrow—early. I haven't seen Ginny *and* Tramp for about a week, and video chat just isn't the same. My friends don't understand what is happening to me—I hardly do myself—and prior to tonight I have no doubt they've talked about taking me to the hospital again, but I don't care.

I leave the restaurant, where we've rung in the new year, at one o'clock and I must say my friends are in rare form. When the clock struck midnight, Niccolò—Nico for short—

kissed Hugh. Nico is much younger, good-looking in that exotic Mediterranean way. He's slim and fit, too well-dressed and too well-groomed for the average heterosexual man. He's Italian, but the kiss was undoubtedly French. The two of them have been lip-locked in a corner ever since. Hugh is probably going to wonder about this tomorrow.

Matt is doing a horrible Magic Mike slash Miley Cyrus imitation, but most of all he looks like Jim (Jason Biggs) stripping for Nadia (Shannon Elizabeth) in 'American Pie.' That movie is from 1999, by the way. Matt is standing on a table and wiggling his ass like he's getting paid for it. He's wearing socks, his shirt is open, his tie is around his neck, and he's wearing too small blue and orange striped Calvin Klein briefs. His jeans are currently on the floor on the men's toilet and that's a horrible place for *anything* to be. Really. I have no idea where his shoes are. Amazingly, there's a crowd of women around the table, filming and looking up at his pale flesh and complete lack of rhythm. I wonder if he'll get paid. I truly hope so, because he'll probably need the money for the lawsuit from Calvin when the videos go online.

Jeff is performing multiple surgeries at the same time on a woman wearing a blue metallic tinsel wig. A tonsil removal with his togue. A mammogram without the X-ray with his left hand. And under the table something that looks an awful lot like a transvaginal examination without the ultrasound with his right hand. Up until now, I'd say he was lying, but he really *can* multitask. I'm actually rather impressed.

Pete is playing dart—too drunk to be interested in women, but apparently sober enough to throw darts…somewhere.

I feel almost relieved when I step into the street. I feel like running all the way home, but the crowds on the pavement makes it impossible. I sidestep people and vomit and firecrackers and it feels so strange looking at the celebrations and not being in the middle of it like I've usually been. I also feel strange because Tramp is usually with me when I walk through the city at night. I'm not afraid or uneasy, it just feels strange I'm alone. By pain of death, I'm not admitting that to anyone. Particularly not Tramp.

Do you know the movie 'I am Legend' from 2007? It starred Will Smith as Robert Neville. Equally important it starred two German Shepherds—Abbey and Kona—who played Neville's dog Sam. The movie is a post-apocalyptic action thriller and the zombies are sophisticated enough to be called 'nocturnal mutants.'

January first, I drive to Ginny's house. Fast. I leave home at six in the morning and the city is mostly deserted. The few lunatics milling around could easily pass for zombies— excuse me…nocturnal humans.

It's raining and still dark when I get to Ginny's place. The outdoor lights are on and she sees me coming. She opens the door for Tramp, who storms out the door towards me. I get down on my knee, that way I won't be tackled to the ground. Like this, it's only my one knee getting wet—in theory at least.

It's been a week since I saw Ginny and I probably greet her with the same enthusiasm Tramp greeted me. Only I don't wag my ass like crazy and knock her over like Tramp just did me. I kiss her—thoroughly—and I hold her close. My jacket is wet but she doesn't seem to mind when she hugs me as fiercely as I do her.

The kitchen smells of coffee and bacon and we sit down for breakfast.

"So, did everyone survive New Year's Eve?" Ginny asks, and I nod as I chew on a piece of bacon.

"Matt became a stripper, Jeff a surgeon, Hugh bisexual, and Pete gave up on women. How did you do?" I ask as Ginny starts laughing.

"A surgeon? That sounds dangerous."

"It wasn't," I say and shake my head. "He used both hands and his tongue. At the same time. He *can* actually multitask."

"I'm impressed."

"I don't think he can do it sober, though."

"Tramp chased a firecracker. He caught it too, but fortunately, he also fell into the pond." I draw a breath of relief, but I don't blame Ginny. Tramp is—and probably always will be—a little bit out of control, hence the disclaimer. With him you can't predict everything, believe me I've tried.

After breakfast, Ginny clears the table and I'm reminded of the first night I came to visit, how desperate I had been to touch her when she was standing by the kitchen table. And now I can. I get up and wrap my arms around her. I kiss the side of her neck and hold her close. She feels amazing and when she sighs and leans back against me, I'm a very happy man. With a very happy cock.

"Care to start the new year with me in bed?" I ask. She turns, smiles, and kisses me, and I think her answer is going to be yes. Only it isn't—imagine that!

"No. We need to talk, Simon," she says. That doesn't bode well, does it? Only she looks more happy than angry, so I'm guessing this can't be a bad thing. Not *too* bad anyway.

"Okay?" She gestures towards the table, and I sit down on the blue wooden chair. It's not very comfortable, but now I know that this house is almost a museum for Ginny's working-class family I like it a little better. She sits down on the other side of the table and she looks like she has to pull herself together.

"I'm pregnant. At least the first test says so." She's looking calm, but defiant, and I sense the angry woman, I met at the park, is lurking just beneath the surface.

"You are?" My brain is struggling to accept this. I knew it was a risk, but I just didn't give a shite at the time.

"I'm keeping the baby Simon."

"Yeah, okay." Brain is still struggling.

"You don't have to do anything."

"I-I want to." Brain has rebooted, funny and unknown feeling is spreading in my chest.

"I'm thirty, Simon, I'm not waiting around for Prince Charming."

"What the hell am I, then?" I object.

"More like Flynn Rider," she says drily. I have absolutely no idea who she's talking about. "You should watch Tangled," she explains at my blank stare. "Watch it with Tramp. I'm certain he can relate to Maximus."

"It's a dog?"

"It's a horse." Close enough. Tramp wags his tail like he's totally on board with this idea. Probably about officially being a horse too.

"Who's Flynn Rider then?"

"Just watch it, the smoulder is very much you." I guess I'll be watching Tangled.

"I have no clue if this is a good thing," I say hesitantly.

"It might be."

I look at her while my brain struggles to process what she's just told me—and I'm not talking about the tangled thing. Not the movie at least. But I really shouldn't be surprised, should I? Remember I told you I fucked Ginny so many times it'd be a miracle if she didn't get pregnant? Well, apparently, she did. And *that* somehow feels like a miracle.

Do you know the song 'Miracles' by Pet Shop Boys? It's from 2003 and sung by Neil Tennant. It's a great song—even Tramp likes it. And I like Pet Shop Boys far better than Bee Gees. Anyway, I've always found the lyrics a bit too poetic for my taste, but suddenly, the parts about greener grass, sunlight, and bluer sky makes sense to me. Remember I told you I was never having children? Well, apparently, I am.

"You know what *is* a good thing?" I finally ask Ginny. "You getting pregnant."

"Really?" She asks warily, and I nod.

"Yeah." My heart is pounding, I don't feel brave at all, but I feel happy. Hopefully bravery will come later. So far, I've survived Tramp—how bad can a baby be? At least they don't eat thongs. Not that I'm aware of at least.

"You look a little scared," she says dubiously.

"Shouldn't I be?"

"With your genes? Probably."

"Hey," I object but suddenly I see opportunity! "Margot will have an anxiety attack," I say delighted and I can't help grinning. She's going to freak out at the thought of a small new Simon lose in the world, I'm certain. Yet another reason this baby is a miracle.

I get up from the chair and gently pull Ginny to her feet. She's got the most amazing green eyes and I know I want her to keep looking up at me like this with that soft look on her face—probably forever. At least that what it feels like right now.

"Do you remember when we talked about drunk me and sober me?"

"When you showed me your bedroom for the first time?" I nod and I can't help smiling. Ginny might've commented on The Good the Bad and the Ugly poster to begin with, but later we investigated how *good* it could be when I was really *bad*. It was very good indeed. We skipped the ugly.

"Well, as it happens sober me know something important."

"Really?" She looks unimpressed, she shouldn't be.

"Sober me knows I'm in love with you." Her eyes widen slightly. My heart is pounding, because this feels like the most important moment of my life so far.

"You are?" I nod. "I am too." It's barely a whisper, but I hear her loud and clear. By now I've given up trying to sort out the unknown feeling I have. I don't give a shite right now.

"Really?" I ask. I know I look bloody amazing, but love is another thing entirely, isn't it? Ginny nods.

"I don't just let any idiot into my bed. Particularly not without a condom."

"I hope this baby won't have any fur."

"You should still watch Tangled, though," she insists.

*

I'm watching Tangled and hell…I might want to change my name to Flynn—not accepting Eugene, no way. I also might want to give Tramp a new name: Maximus. Maximus, the horse, eats paper too by the way.

Do you know the movie 'Tangled' from 2010? I do too now. It's the 50th Disney animated movie based on the fairy-tale Rapunzel by the Brothers Grimm. The script is written by

Dan Fogelman. The story is about the long-lost princess Rapunzel, who yearns to leave the confines of her secluded tower. Against her foster mother's wishes, she makes a deal with a *handsome* intruder, Flynn Rider, to take her out into the world she has never seen. The *handsome* intruder is voiced by Zachary Levi. He looks okay—Flynn does too—but, honestly, have you seen *me*? Of course, some idiot decided to make Tangled into a television series too—fifty-nine horrible episodes because apparently you can't let any movie go unspoiled if there's the slightest chance of earning more money.

For some stupid reason, I invited Pete, Jeff, Hugh and Matt to watch Tangled with me. Hugh and Jeff have already seen it, and I just hate the smug look on Hugh's face every time Flynn says *anything*. Hugh watches *me* more than he watches the TV. When Flynn says, "Super human good looks, I've always had them," they all burst out laughing while I rack my brain, because I'm certain I've said that at some point. Or at least I've thought it. I now have four friends—adult, male friends—who can pretty much quote the *entire* movie. The *entire* one hour and forty minutes movie. Including the songs. I hate the singing—both my friends and in the movie.

"Here comes the smoulder." Pete is about to kill himself by laughter every single time he says this.

"Your smoulder broke when you met Ginny," Hugh guffaws. I don't understand why he hasn't hurt himself laughing. Honestly, he should have pulled at least a few muscles by now.

"Fifty says I can break your smoulder too," I snap.

"Try me."

"I'll take that bet," Matt says.

"You still owe me a hundred," Jeff complains.

"You'll get half in a moment."

"Go on then," Hugh says.

"Ginny's pregnant."

Someone give me a bloody pin—along with all the money I've just won. I'd be able to hear the pin drop even if I threw it out the window from the fourth floor. Tramp looks at us, clearly very confused about what's going on. One moment the living room was noisy—and he was being petted—and now it's quiet as the grave. And nobody's petting him.

"Yeah, I'd say Simon won that one," Pete says drily.

"Pay up, assholes," I say and hold out my hand.

"She's really pregnant?" Jeff asks and I nod. They just look at me, and I anticipate another conversation where they consider if they need to take me to the hospital. Come to think of it, they're probably going to offer me a fake passport and a ride to the airport.

"I'm going to be a bloody uncle," Hugh roars and gets up from the couch like someone pushed his internal eject button. He hugs me fiercely and when he pulls away from me, I swear his eyes are glistening. "I'm going to be an uncle!" he roars again, clearly delighted, and Tramp barks happily—*finally* someone has started making noise again. Matt whistles enthusiastically—he still needs to work on that compared to Ginny—and Pete and Jeff hug each other like they've got any credit in the pregnancy.

We jump up and down like idiots, like hooligans would do if their team had just won…hell if I know, but something important. Tramp jumps around with us, he barks happily, and my bet is he'll blame my friends if we get a noise complaint. He's smart like that.

"Ahem…" We all freeze and turn to the doorway. Ginny is standing there, grocery bags in hand, and she looks at us like she really wants to know what we're doing—or not. As the only bright person in the room, Tramp whines delighted and runs to greet her. I straighten my hair, Hugh coughs delicately, Pete waves stupidly, and Jeff looks to the ceiling. I suspect he'll start whistling innocently in a moment. Matt on the other hand rushes to Ginny and takes the bags from her.

"You're pregnant, you shouldn't carry that," he says and looks at me judgementally. Ginny looks at him. Then she looks at me. And then she smiles.

Do you know the movie 'Alice in Wonderland' from 2010? It's based on the book by Lewis Carroll and this particular version is a Tim Burton film. Tim Burton, and you just know you are in for a visual treat. And then there is the cast…Johnny Depp, Helena Bonham Carter, Anne Hathaway, Crispin Glover among others. And that's only the beginning. Voices by Michael Sheen, Stephen Fry, Alan Rickman and Christopher Lee—I could talk about this forever. The visuals and the voices are great, but all in all the movie is rubbish and I just barely prefer it to the 1951 version by Disney. That, by the way, was the 13th release of Disney's animated features. But there is *one thing*—one *single* thing—Disney nailed far better than Burton, and that's the Cheshire Cat and particularly its smile. Burton's looked like it needed a dentist—Disney's became legend.

And that smile—the Cheshire Cat's smile—is what spreads across Ginny's face this very moment. I'm so fucked. There's no easy way to say it, no nice way to say it either. I. Am. Fucked. Which, of course, means my friends are fucked too. There, now I feel better.

*

In case you are wondering…slavery still exists. In our day of age, it's called manipulation—and stupid men. Also, Ginny cooks for them and in case you'd like to know…yes, men *are* that easy. There are two ways to a man's heart—his cock or his stomach. Yes, really. Because of her cooking and comparing me to Flynn Rider, Ginny has practically been crowned queen by my friends. I can't say I'm unhappy about this, because it would've been horrible, if they didn't like her. We tried that a few years ago when Pete almost forced us all into a new version of 'Saving Silverman.' Ironically, his 'Judith' was called Amanda, and she made Amanda Peet look like a fun-loving angel. If you don't know what I'm talking about you should *not* watch the 2001 movie. I recommend you don't. Besides, men are not *that* stupid. Probably not anyway.

There's only *one* thing about Ginny's pregnancy I don't like. If Tramp wasn't such a bastard, I wouldn't have been at the park early in the morning—and I probably wouldn't have met Ginny. He probably *is* Pongo at matchmaking—at least humans. I've not admitted it to him and I'm not going to either.

There's also *one* thing about my friends liking Ginny I don't appreciate. They're here constantly. The size of my apartment was fine when I was alone. Add Tramp and it became crowded. Add Ginny and it became cluttered. I've never realised how much I appreciated my forced minimalism until now. I don't mind her crowding my bed though. Not at all. Add four grown men and the apartment is starting to feel like rush hour in Japan. But the worst part is, my eternal bachelor and *very* single friends have suddenly become experts on relationships and women you keep longer than a single night—meaning they question everything I say or do concerning Ginny. Today is apparently no exception.

"Are you going to marry her?" Hugh asks and looks at me critically.

"You should," Matt says and nods like he's suddenly become the voice of reason. He's not, he never will be, and if it ever happens that means the Armageddon is here and it's all over for us anyway. So please, let us all listen to Matt.

"Illegitimate child," Pete chides.

"So? This isn't the nineteen fifties," I protest.

"Tsk tsk tsk," Jeff says and shakes his head like he too is disappointed in me.

"Tramp should carry the rings," Matt says.

"I should be best man," Hugh determines.

"No!" Jeff shouts. "You already claimed uncle, you can't be best man too." He looks genuinely upset by this and gets up from his chair. Hugh gets up too and suddenly they're nose to nose.

"Frodo," I call loudly. I wait, but Tramp doesn't come into the living room.

"What the hell are you doing?" Matt asks. He looks at me like *I'm* the one who's gone insane.

"Tramp doesn't respond to Frodo, he has just disqualified himself as ringbearer," I dismiss.

"You are an idiot," Matt says and then joins the loud discussion Jeff, Hugh and Pete are having. I rub my face. We are moments from a pub fight, but I let it unfold for my own entertainment. Sounds like they're teaming up against Hugh, because apparently, he can't claim uncle *and* best man just because he's smarter and faster than the rest of them put together. Amidst the shouting, I also hear Hugh blaming me I' haven't proposed to Ginny yet.

Truth is I already asked Ginny to marry me. I bought her a ring, got down on one knee and everything. I'm sure there's a movie for the perfect proposal too, but every time I thought about it my head got stuck with Elisabeth Bennet and Mr Darcy. Embarrassing really, because that is *Margot's* favourite—definitely not mine—but she has forced me to watch it a million times. In case you are wondering, we *are* talking about the 1995 BBC series with Colin Firth and Jennifer Ehle. Of course, we are. Firth rose to stardom, Helen Fielding wrote Bridget Jones novels, someone mistakenly made a movie in 2005, and Margot's obsession keeps on living.

I blamed Margot—loudly—for infecting my brain with Mr Darcy. His first proposal was horrible, the second of no use to me, so she deserved the blame. She started blabbering some nonsense about not being able to fix on the hour, or the spot, or the look, or the words, which laid the foundation. It was too long ago. And something about being in the middle before knowing that I *had* begun. That last part might be true, because I have no idea when I started falling in love with Ginny. I know it wasn't the first time we met, not the second time either. But from there on, I'm pretty much at a loss. I'm almost tempted to say that dogs can do that to you, but in this case it's *women* can do that to you. One particular woman, to be precise. So, I skipped the theatrical, the dramatic, the complex, and the imitations, and went for short and sweet and honesty. And I didn't even make any inappropriate comments. I was very proud and I secretly think Ginny was too.

She still said no, though. Imagine that!

Truth is, I *want* to get married. Imagine that too! So, I'm not done asking, I'll wear her down. I can easily imagine it, and one day I'll be telling you that after years and years of asking, and asking, and asking, she finally said yes. The party lasted an entire week, and honestly, I don't remember much of it.

Ginny curiously pokes her head into the living room to see what the commotion is all about. I get up and go to her. Tramp is right beside her as he always is these days.

"What's going on?"

"They're planning our wedding."

"Oh," she says. She's completely unfazed, but I suppose she's gotten used to them by now. And it's going to take more than four additional idiots to change Ginny's mind about anything.

"And arguing about who can be uncle and the best man. And Matt wants Tramp to be Frodo."

"You mean carry the ring?" I smile and nod. At least somebody understands me!

Just to be clear…If you don't understand the Frodo reference, I'm not having anything to do with you until you've watched Peter Jackson's 'Lord of the Rings' trilogy—extended version of course. Numerous times. Including *all* of the bonus material. Numerous times. It was released in 2021 in a 4K version by the way and I *do* recommend it.

Ginny is now five months pregnant and her belly is beautiful and I lay my hand on it every time I'm near her. It's cute and round and I only *once* made the mistake of telling her she looked more bloated than pregnant. She's wearing an apron because she started spilling on it. She often has a drop of sauce on her stomach, but I don't think that's the only reason Tramp loves it. His love for her—and her stomach with sauce—has grown just like she has. His new favourite thing is Ginny's stomach. He stares at it, he sniffs it, he pokes it gently with his snout, and lays his head on it constantly. When we're walking, he never strays far from her, he doesn't give a shite about me as always.

"Exactly," I say and smile at her. I'm certain it's a loving smile, because which man wouldn't love a woman, who understands Frodo references?

"We could just elope?" She says. I glance at Tramp, who looks at me expectantly like he's waiting to be included in whatever it is we're contemplating. I groan loudly because I know we can't take Tramp to the Caribbean to get married. Remember when I told you dog owners are crazy? Well, that still stands because apparently, I want Tramp to be at the wedding. And that means no Caribbean. If you would just excuse me for a moment, I'm going to kill myself.

"Can you still get married at Gretna Green?" At least we can drive there.

"Ugh, Simon, that was not was I was thinking, when I was talking about elopement."

"I know, but…" I glance at Tramp and Ginny groans.

"You don't want to get married without Tramp."

"Yes!" I say too fast and too loud. "No," I admit. Tramp sits down beside me. He looks up at me and I swear there's love in his eyes. At least that's what I tell myself. Maybe he loves me because he's gotten his way again. Told you, my dog is an asshole.

Ginny sticks two fingers in her mouth and whistles. It's so loud it resonates in the entire apartment. Tramp stands to attention, and the four idiots who were arguing amazingly stops shouting, and Jeff even let go of Hugh's collar. Moments away from a pub fight—told you.

"You can't whistle for shite, Matt," Pete says and looks at Ginny, clearly impressed.

"What are you doing?" Ginny demands.

"Hugh can't be uncle *and* best man," Jeff says aggressively.

"It's not fair," Pete complains like grown men are toddlers. Wait a minute…we are.

"The hell I can," Hugh argues and this earns him another killing look from Jeff.

"Best man? What are you talking about?" Ginny demands.

"He should marry you," Matt, the new voice of reason, says. We are all doomed.

"Who says he didn't ask me? Who says I accepted?" Ginny inquires and I cringe. My friends look at each other. Hugh's wearing a knitted red sweater, Pete a purple T-shirt, Jeff a blue sweatshirt, and Matt an orange T-shirt that probably matches the too small blue and orange striped Calvin Klein briefs he wore on New Year's Eve. Their clothing almost makes them look like the 'Teenage Mutant Ninja Turtles'—the cringe-worthy 1990 version of course—plotting their next pizza order. Then they look at me and I just know they're going to ridicule me for the rest of my life. I asked her, she said no.

"She broke your smoulder," Hugh says and they all start laughing like it's the funniest shite they've ever heard. Ginny quirks an eyebrow but none of them see it because they're too busy laughing.

Their laughing turns to arguing again. Hugh is in trouble, and Ginny and I stand in the living room like we're watching an absurd episode of something that could be either a comedy or reality TV. I'm a little distraught I don't have anything to compare it to, but in general I like movies—not endless episodes of something stupid dying too slowly. At least a bad movie ends after a couple of hours.

"That's it," Ginny says exasperated and shakes her head. "None of them are going to be *anything*." They all stop arguing and turn towards her with looks of horror I've only seen when I've told Tramp there'll be no food for him. I'm pretty sure Ginny's not going to feed them either—starting today. She turns and walks to the kitchen and *The Turtles* run after her no doubt desperate for her to change her mind. Ironically, Ginny's making pizza for dinner tonight.

I sit down on the couch and put my feet on the living room table. For once, Tramp chooses me over Ginny, and he sits down beside me and lays his head in my lap. I scratch his ear and smile as I hear loud voices from the kitchen where The Turtles object to Ginny's statement. Tramp doesn't mind, he probably knows too they're no match for her. Their objections turn to begging and pleading and I feel my smile turn sinister. If they continue like that, I'm going to be the next Willem Dafoe!

My future wife—hopefully—is in the kitchen, cooking and intimidating my friends. My dog likes me—at least at the moment—and I've secured the next generation to terrorise my sister. And now, I finally know what that funny and unknown feeling was. It is the feeling of my new dream.

--- THE END ---

Milton Keynes UK
Ingram Content Group UK Ltd.
UKHW020626151123
432605UK00010B/264